SUMMER BOYS

HAILEY ABBOTT

SCHOLASTIC INC.

New York   Toronto   London   Auckland   Sydney
Mexico City   New Delhi   Hong Kong   Buenos Aires

ISBN 0-439-54020-8

Copyright © 2004 by 17th Street Productions, an Alloy, Inc. company
All rights reserved. Published by Scholastic Inc.

ALLOYENTERTAINMENT

Produced by Alloy Entertainment
151 West 26th Street
New York, NY 10001

SCHOLASTIC and associated logos are trademarks and/or registered trademarks of Scholastic Inc.

Book design by Steve Scott
The text type was set in Bulmer.

12 11 10 9   6 7 8 9/ 0

Printed in the U.S.A.
First printing, June 2004

For Texas Will

1

Jamie Tuttle unhooked the clasp of her platinum locket and laid it on the dresser. Then she picked up a beaded necklace and slipped that on instead. The locket was something her mom had given her on her sixteenth birthday, and it contained a picture of Jamie as a little girl. But Ethan had given Jamie the beaded necklace at the end of last summer, and just wearing it made her pulse spike. She couldn't believe that within half an hour she'd be standing next to the guy. At last.

Swiveling, Jamie faced the mirror and gave herself a once-over. She was wearing a drawstring skirt she'd sewn herself and an off-the-shoulder cotton top she'd bought at the Salvation Army. Jamie noticed now that the pale green quilting on the skirt brought out the darker green in her eyes, and the effect contrasted nicely with the brown freckles dusting her nose. She'd never felt prettier. Then she pulled out the rubber band from her black hair and watched as the curls poofed out around her face, expanding like Chinese noodles dropped in a fryer. She frowned.

"I look like a lion."

She had already tried wetting her hands and patting down the curls that refused to behave. Now she put her hands on her hips and tilted her head to the side, considering. Maybe lion wasn't quite right. She looked like the picture on the cover of a book she'd read once, *Julie of the Wolves*.

"I can't believe you can feel this bad about hair," she said to the mirror Jamie. The mirror Jamie understood that Jamie was not a girl who cared about hair. No, this was a girl who practically invented the messy bun look and chose to wear Chap Stick instead of lipstick, because Chap Stick didn't require a cosmetic mirror to put on.

"Whatever," Jamie said dismissively, grabbing her tiny, beaded purse and hurrying down the hallway of her aunt and uncle's summer cottage. She was so psyched to see Ethan.

"I'm going to the pier," she called to her uncle, who was in the den.

"Have fun," he said, his eyes on the Dodgers game on TV.

Jamie stepped out onto the stoop and rubbed her feet on the mat. Every time the Tuttles — five adults and seven cousins — invaded this part of Maine, it took less than an hour for the sand to invade the three houses they rented each year. The sand was always sticking to their feet and sneaking into the fabric of the chairs and couches and rugs. As she ran her soles along the short, wiry fibers, Jamie remembered something from previous summers — that she loved the feeling of the sand in between her toes, but she loved the feeling of rubbing it off, too. She made a mental note to herself to write that down in her journal. Jamie fancied herself an up-and-coming writer and had made a personal vow to keep a detailed list of everything and anything that inspired her.

Jamie could hear Uncle Carr's kids, Jordan, Jessi, and Drew, squealing and laughing in the backyard. She took a huge breath and strode outside, sucking in the familiar sights along with the fresh, salty air. She, her uncle, her aunt, and her three little cousins had gotten in an hour ago, but she already felt like they'd never left Pebble Beach. Here, at the edge of the dirt road that led to the pier, were the three little white cottages Jamie's extended family rented every summer for seven weeks. Parents, uncles, aunts, cousins, and friends would be coming and going all summer long. It was like their own private oceanside compound, and had been that way since Jamie was a kid. Jamie always stayed with her dad's younger brother and his wife, since they were both teachers and had the summers off. Jamie's own parents could only come up from New Jersey when they could get away from work.

Jamie debated stopping at the other cottages to see if anyone was still around. But she was too eager to get to the party at the pier. Her mind was running Ethan on a constant reel, and her heart was in her throat. She hurried down the path.

There was a figure up ahead under the trees. It was getting dark outside but the shapely figure could only mean one person. "El?" Jamie called.

Ella turned and craned her neck. "Hey!" She bounded back and wrapped her arms around Jamie's neck. She smelled like lilacs and coconut Body Butter. "It's great to see you! You look fabulous! How was your ride up?"

Ella pulled back and beamed. Jamie's cousin — the daughter of her father's oldest brother — always looked fantastic. This

3

summer, her blonde hair fell down the sides of her face in clean, choppy layers, and she'd gotten long bangs, which made her look kind of hipsterish. Her cheeks were rosy from the sun and dusted with some kind of bronzer that made her skin shine. She was wearing an impossibly short, sheathy sundress with a low neckline and razor-thin straps that showed off her smooth, straight shoulders and perfect cleavage. She looked a little like one of the Hilton sisters, only less skinny and without the obnoxious factor.

"It wasn't too bad. Uncle Carr drove like a psycho, and we had to stop seven times because Jessi had to pee. That little kid has the weakest bladder of anyone I know," Jamie said.

Ella's laugh was snorty, like a kid's. Jamie sometimes felt intimidated by Ella at first — she was an Übergirl, the kind that you might see leading a pack of hoochie-mama dancers in a hip-hop video. Jamie was the opposite — straight and thin, her figure more like Avril than Christina. But Ella could be goofy, too.

"I was just on my way to the pier," Ella said, her brown eyes dancing.

"I figured," Jamie said, letting Ella link an arm through hers and pull her into motion.

"Let's dig up some cuties tonight." Ella squeezed Jamie's wrist affectionately with her fingers.

"El, I already have a boyfriend." Jamie grinned. "Ethan, remember?"

Ella raised her eyebrows. "The guy from last summer?"

"Mm-hmm."

"Whoa, you guys are still together?"

Jamie smiled at Ella's look of total shock. It *was* kind of incredible — a whole year of a long-distance relationship, based on two little months at the beach. A whole year of letters, phone calls, e-mails. Jamie had spent the past year looking through and over guys back home, always focusing on *this* summer and being back with Ethan. But it hadn't seemed like a sacrifice. There was no contest between him and anyone else because Ethan understood Jamie in a way that no one else had. He was her best friend.

"What about you? Are you dating anyone?" Jamie asked, hoping that their chat wouldn't last a second longer. Ethan was only minutes away.

Ella drew a breath, and then listed the guys she was interested in at the moment, casually waving one hand in the air in a you-know-how-it-is-to-be-adored-by-too-many-men-at-once gesture. Jamie listened intently. Though it was completely foreign to her, she loved that Ella went through boys quicker than a pack of Dentyne Ice (Ella was a chain chewer). She also seemed to have so much confidence, which Jamie really admired. In fact, Jamie had already written down in her trusty journal that a girl like Ella would make the perfect heroine in her debut novel.

The dirt road ended in a paved street lined with cottages, where the girls turned left and headed toward the shore. Once they were walking parallel to the ocean, they could see the pier up ahead, strung with tiny white lights and packed with people. The sounds of the party drifted toward them on the breeze — people laughing, live music. As they got closer, Jamie scanned the crowd for Ethan. She craned her neck as they slid into the crowd at the pier's base. Suddenly, a pair of arms engulfed her. But they belonged to a girl.

Ella's older sister, Kelsi, pulled back far enough to grin at Jamie. "We were wondering when you'd show up," she said. "George has been staring wistfully down the beach all afternoon."

Jamie laughed as her other cousin Beth and Beth's friend George piled in for a hug.

"I've been waiting patiently, sweet cheeks," George added.

He pinched Jamie's waist and Jamie pinched him back. George, who'd come with Beth last summer and was staying with her now, was always teasing the girls, but it meant nothing. He was like their surrogate brother.

"And we all know how patient boys with ADD can be," Beth added. Beth was tall, lean, and sinewy — the most athletic of all the cousins. Her hair was blonde, though a few shades darker than Ella's (their dads, who were brothers, were both flaxen-haired). And unlike Ella, Beth usually wore her hair plain and straight, brushed off her face and pulled back in a ponytail. Tonight, it was covered by a ratty baseball cap, and she wore an old high school gym T-shirt and jogging shorts. Jamie always thought Beth, with her full lips and blue eyes, was really pretty in a natural way, but she knew that if she told her cousin that, Beth would just laugh it off. She wasn't one to care much about looks.

"I think we saw your lover man from last year up near the stage," Kelsi said as she ran her fingers through her short blonde hair. "That guy from last year. Ian?"

Jamie's throat constricted.

"Actually, his name is Ethan," she corrected, and then pulled away. She tried to glimpse the area by the stage, but the pier was just too packed.

"I'll be right back," she said, drifting away.

Jamie picked at her beaded necklace as she wove her way down the pier, feeling like maybe this was the happiest moment she could ever remember having. She pictured Ethan's face — the tiny scar on his chin, the waves of his light brown hair. And then there he was, his head bobbing to the music coming from the band on stage. Jamie would know the distinctive curve of the back of his neck anywhere. She ran the last couple of feet and ducked against his back, so that when he swiveled his head, he couldn't see her face. She jabbed her index fingers into his back like tiny guns.

"We're gonna walk out of here very slowly," she said in a deep voice. "Once we get outside, you're going to take all your clothes off. No funny business, got it?"

Ethan burst out laughing. He turned to face her and made a fake look of surprise. Then he reached down and picked her up, planting his lips on hers at the same time her feet left the ground.

Jamie felt a spring inside her uncoil and relax as Ethan kissed her. She let herself melt into the warmth of his body. She breathed in how good he smelled and pulled back to get a better look at him. *Yep, still absolutely gorgeous,* she thought, as she flashed him an uncontrollable smile. She'd forgotten how he looked much older than seventeen. She'd forgotten the aroma of his shampoo, but now it came back to her — the spicy-sweet fragrance of Bed Head.

Jamie wondered what else she'd forgotten, and she couldn't wait to start remembering. It was going to be a great summer.

2

As she hovered on the edge of the circle that she, Kelsi, Beth, and George had made, Ella inserted her fingers into her neckline and tugged it down so that her perky breasts stood out a little bit more. Restless, her eyes scanned the pier, scoping for interesting boys. She wished she had a drink in her hand. Or a cigarette. Anything to make her appear older and more sophisticated. She just had this antsy feeling, like she was standing in a long line outside of a hot, trendy club in New York City, anxiously waiting for the bouncer at the door to look at her fake ID and let her in. Or maybe she was just tense because she was missing her underwear. She'd left it lying on her bed back at the cottage in an act of "I'm going commando" rebellion against Kelsi, who'd insisted the thong was too skimpy for such a short skirt.

In fact, Ella had been getting that "something's missing" feeling a lot lately. This party was the perfect example. Last year, it had been the highlight. Ella had thrived on the crowd — all the boys with their slightly sun-kissed skin, and the unforgettable taste of the start of summer. This year, however, the festivities felt smaller and less exciting.

"Hey, mind if I bum one of those?" she asked, turning to a guy standing and smoking directly behind the group, who was cute in an all-American, Chris Klein kind of way. He reached into his pocket, his eyes gliding along Ella's figure as they rose to meet hers. Then he handed her a pack of Marlboro Lights. Ella gave him a faint smile, took a cigarette, and tucked it into the corner of her gloss-covered lips. He extended his lighter and she leaned forward, watching his eyes dart down to her chest. Ella wanted to laugh. Boys were so predictable.

"Thanks," she said coolly. She turned back toward Beth, George, and Kelsi. Ignoring her sister's look of disapproval, Ella blew a cloud of smoke into the air and rejoined the conversation.

"So Jamie's in love, huh?" Beth asked the group while turning to see whether Jamie and Ethan were visible in the crowd that was gathered near the stage.

"I think I'm going to get a boyfriend this summer," Ella mused out loud in reply, pretty much dismissing the current topic. She hadn't really thought about it before this second, but suddenly it sounded right.

"El, I thought you had, like, ten boyfriends," George put in.

"More 'slaves,'" Beth made air quotes with her fingers, "than 'boyfriends.'"

Ella shrugged. It was sort of true. She smirked and thought of all the hot guys back home who really liked how fickle she was. They were most attracted to her whenever her attention started to drift (which could happen in ten minutes flat if they weren't careful). She tapped the cigarette ash.

"Well, I just want *one* now. From now on, my motto is 'Learn to love commitment.'" Ella nodded. It sounded good.

"El, that's impossible," Kelsi said flatly. "You're not that kind of girl."

Ella shot a dirty look at Kelsi, who was a taller, earthier version of herself. Kelsi was only a year and a half older, but if one sister was prettier than the other, it was only by the shade of a fraction. Still, wherever they went, it was Ella who got the attention. Ella was the one who sparkled and dazzled, while Kelsi was the one who didn't wear makeup and smelled like patchouli. So Kelsi, who couldn't really understand what it was like to get distracted by so many boys at once, had a tendency to act all judgmental around her little sister. But Ella couldn't help it. She *wanted* to be satisfied, but every time she had something (or someone) in her possession, she'd soon find something else that was more interesting and move on.

"I'm gonna take a walk," Ella said through a sigh, and trotted toward the gaggle of girls and boys who were hanging out by the water. She was bored with just standing around, and mingling with strangers might help her decide which guy back home would be a good candidate for a boyfriend. Eric, Jeff, Josh, the other Jeff? The possibilities were endless.

The crowd was thick, but not so much that Ella couldn't feel the cool evening breeze on her skin. She brushed her bangs out of her eyes and already she could feel the salt air saturating her golden locks, making each strand grainy and thick. She squeezed through knots of surfer dudes, a bunch of tube-top-clad girls dancing in a clump, a college-age couple with their arms circling each other's waists. A few guys tried to talk to Ella while she strolled along, but none of them impressed her. She took a long, blasé drag on her cigarette to underline this point to everyone.

But then she had to pause mid-exhale.

Up on the stage, the band was rocking. In Ella's opinion, they weren't particularly good, but they were trying. The drummer had spiked-out blue hair and wiry arms that flung themselves against the drums so hard, she could see the vibrations shooting up and down his lean muscles. The two guitarists were thrashing around as if angry bees were trapped in their pants.

But it was the lead singer who grabbed Ella's attention. He had black hair and dark, almond-shaped eyes. He effortlessly stroked the strings of his black electric guitar, which rested against his pelvis in an almost forgetting-it-was-there kind of way. His mouth clung so close to the microphone that he was almost French kissing it while he sang. Ella was mesmerized. Her mouth went dry and she couldn't stop biting her lower lip. He was beautiful, and the ultrahip vibe he was giving off was completely irresistible.

She pushed her way to the edge of the stage and tried to make eye contact with the singer, all the while very conscious of her body and how soft it was, and how great her breasts looked in her dress. Although she started dancing to the music in an attempt to get his attention, he didn't look down at her. After the song crashed around lopsidedly for another few minutes, it suddenly came to a grinding stop. The singer held his hand up in a casual wave and whispered into the microphone, "Thanks. We're done."

Then he did something that took Ella's breath away. He pulled off his T-shirt, unveiling a smooth brown chest with a light dusting of hair across his pecs. He strode to the left of the stage and went down to the pier, where he hopped right off the edge, rising gracefully for a second in the air, almost levitating, and then disappearing into the water below. As the other members of the band followed, the audience cheered them on. Ella and several others ran to the edge of the pier and leaned over. She watched the boys surface, their heads bobbing up and down in the water as they swam back to shore.

Ella's laugh bubbled up out of her. The feeling of restlessness was gone. This guy was something completely new. He seemed flawless.

She dashed back toward the beach so that she could be the first person to greet him when he came out of the water.

"I thought you were gonna grow your hair even longer to look like a pirate," Ella heard Jamie say.

"I tried but it looked dorky," Ethan replied.

"I bet it looked cute," Jamie cooed sappily.

Ella rolled her eyes, stabbing her toes in between the slats of wood on the pier, and trying to ignore Jamie and Ethan as they were sucked deeper into "The Couple Zone." She was still disappointed that the hottie singer never showed up. When Ella had gotten to the beach, he hadn't been there, and after a long search of the pier, she'd settled near Jamie and her boyfriend by the stage, waiting for the singer to somehow magically resurface there. What else could she do?

The third and headlining band had just finished up, and now there was some lame romantic song playing over the speakers. The sound of Faith Hill crooning was peppered with the occasional kissy noises issuing from Jamie and Ethan. Though Ella was sort of happy for them, she didn't think she could take it any-more. "I think I'm gonna go find Kelsi and head home," she announced. Jamie and Ethan snapped to face her, clearly surprised that she existed.

"Okay, see you later." Jamie's smile was so big, it almost didn't fit on her face.

Ella wove down the pier, occasionally rubbing past other sweaty bodies. Some couples were still dancing, and other people were just standing around talking as the party simmered down. Ella spotted Kelsi near the pier's entrance, perched on the rail with her long skirt hanging between her legs. She was talking to some boy, and her face was flushed and shiny.

The guy with Kelsi reached out and put his hand on her knee, and Ella felt the hairs on the back of her neck stand up as she studied the guy's profile. It was impossible. Could it be?

Kelsi was laughing at something the guy had said when she spotted Ella.

"El!" Kelsi waved Ella over and flashed her a bright smile. "Did you see the band earlier? This guy is . . . Peter, this is my sister, Ella."

Peter, of course, was none other than the hot singer.

Finally, they were making the eye contact Ella had tried for earlier in front of the stage, and she felt her stomach drop.

"Hey," Peter said, giving her a friendly handshake.

Ella enjoyed the feel of his calloused fingertips on her skin. She noticed that he had a tiny, adorable cleft in his chin that made her knees wobbly. But even though she was all caught up in his magnificence, Peter's hand didn't linger in hers. He didn't even glance at her chest or her legs or even so much at her face. He just

13

resumed chatting with Kelsi and gave Ella a nice view of his profile again. Ella's entire body began to feel numb.

"I loved that third song, the one about the space dog," Kelsi enthused, her voice fluttery. Ella tried to remember the words to any of the songs the band had played and came up blank. Perhaps she was too busy processing this insane situation — she was being ignored, and Peter kept touching Kelsi's knee, and Kelsi kept moving and laughing like a natural nonpatchouli flirt, and up close, Peter's vibe was much stronger than she expected.

His bronze skin tone made Ella think that he might be half Polynesian. In fact, Peter resembled a guy Ella had seen in her friend's photos from Tahiti. In the picture, the guy stood in an endless sea of turquoise water, his hands on his hips and beads of moisture dripping off of him. He stared at the camera like he was born to be on the cover of a Chippendales calendar, only not such a pretty boy — just kind of graceful and sexy. Now that Ella thought about it, Peter and Mr. Tahiti could have been identical twins.

As Kelsi and Peter yammered on for several agonizing minutes, Ella continued to stand there, frozen and freaked out. But when Peter's gaze quickly darted her way, she felt a surge of her old confidence and got up the nerve to talk to him.

"You live around here?" she asked, smoothing her tinted lip gloss with her pinky.

Peter nodded, and then shifted his attention back to Kelsi. "Have you guys been down to the Look Out Diner on Hallowell? I'm a short-order cook there."

Ella stepped closer, so she'd be in his line of vision. "Ooh. Do you have pecan pie?"

Peter shrugged. "We might. Why don't you come down and find out?" Again, his remarks seemed to be directed at Kelsi, and Kelsi only.

Ella swallowed. She felt the situation getting away from her. She had to do something drastic — right now.

"Ouch!" Ella screamed and clutched the back of her left thigh.

"What's the matter, El?" Kelsi asked, looking genuinely concerned.

"Damn it! I think something bit me!" Ella whined. She began to limp around in circles.

"Could be a mosquito. They're vicious out here," Peter said.

"Let me take a look," Kelsi said as she approached Ella.

"Okay," Ella whimpered while pulling up her skirt a bit.

Kelsi inspected the lower part of Ella's left thigh and shook her head.

"I don't see anything."

"Well, I know I felt something. It stung like hell," Ella insisted.

Peter closed in on Ella and started peering at her leg.

"Pull your skirt up higher so we can get better look," Kelsi said.

This was working like a charm.

Ella hiked up her dress a tad more, just enough for Peter to get a nice eyeful of her thigh and the teeny heart tattoo she secretly got last summer with that ever-so-wonderful fake ID.

A smile crept over Peter's face when he saw it. "That's an interesting bug bite."

Kelsi, however, was not as amused by her little sister's prank.

"Where did you get that, Ella?" Kelsi demanded.

"What? Don't you like it?"

Kelsi let out a "Hmpf" and yanked down Ella's dress. She leaned over and spoke softly into Ella's ear.

"You little bitch. Just wait until we get home." And with that, Kelsi spun around to Peter.

"Do you feel like going for a walk?" Kelsi asked. "It's such a beautiful night."

Peter replied with a lazy shrug and took Kelsi's elbow. Ella watched their backs as they began to walk down the pier, then glanced down. Her plan hadn't worked out at all. But before she could accept defeat, she heard Peter's voice call out to her, and she looked up

"Hey, Ella," he said over his shoulder. "Tattoos rock!" Then he raised his arm and gave her the devil sign with his hand. Ella responded in kind and even went one step further by sticking out her tongue.

After Kelsi and Peter were out of sight, Ella felt that things were looking brighter. She soaked up the view, which reminded her of another postcard her friend had sent from the same Tahiti trip. It had had an arrow pointing to a lounge chair on the beach, under green-and-brown palm trees. There had been red writing scribbled in at the top, above the arrow: "You should be *here*."

3

"I really don't think this is right."

George stood blinking in the morning sun, his minigolf club dangling between the fingers of his left hand, his right hand scratching the back of his head. He was undoubtedly perplexed.

"No, I don't think I can play this hole," he told Beth.

Beth surveyed the long, slightly curved shape of the green again, and then scanned the sign: HOLE #2: THE DOLPHIN'S FIN. Every respectable minigolf course has a theme, and the one in Pebble Beach was "Circus, Circus!" Above where George and Beth were standing, plaster trapeze artists, decked out in purple tights, walked gingerly through the air. All over the course, shoddy-looking concrete bears and elephants stood forlornly by their corresponding holes. In the far left corner, Beth could just make out the fire hoop that, she knew from years of experience, spit out a tiny flame whenever a ball rolled through it.

George was unhappy because there *were* no dolphins in an actual circus.

"Maybe they're just getting the circus theme confused with a Sea World theme," Beth said thoughtfully. "C'mon, George, let's just play."

George shook his head in defiance. "No, this is just unacceptable. They obviously didn't do their circus research. I'm going to ask for a refund."

Beth rolled her eyes. She knew he was actually considering it. George could take jokes too far, often enough to forget he was joking in the first place. Sometimes, Beth thought, this was an endearing quality, but most times, it was just plain annoying.

"George."

The gauge on Beth's tolerance meter was almost on empty.

George looked at her, resigned. "Okay, okay." He shrugged. "It's just not right, is all. When was the last time you saw a dolphin at the circus? Little kids play minigolf. It's giving them misinformation."

After he finished his diatribe, George shook his shoulders exaggeratedly and lined up the blue ball he'd chosen from the rainbow of colors the cashier had offered. Just across the street and beyond some dunes was the ocean. The wind blew off the water and tousled Beth's blonde hair. She watched George tap his ball. It sailed forward for a moment, then it slowed on a slight rise, approached the hole, and dropped in.

"You're lucky with those blue balls!" Beth shoved George and smiled suggestively, trying to act like she didn't care that he was already winning — she was way over par on this one. True, it would be humiliating to be beaten when she'd been coming here her entire life and George had only visited this course once last summer.

But even though George knew how much his winning was eating Beth up inside, he was nice enough not to gloat (at least, not yet).

They waited while the couple in front of them lollygagged over Hole #3 — the Elephant Trunk. The concrete elephant that stood peering down at them from the other end of the course was skinny and anemic-looking, its gray paint long since turned to a dirty white. The green AstroTurf wove in a long, curvy line, making it almost impossible to get a hole in one unless you lined up your ball perfectly to within a fraction of an inch.

The couple, however, was making it a bigger problem than it had to be. Mostly because they seemed to have no concern whatsoever with actually playing. The girl, a brunette in denim cut-offs, would hit the ball once, and it would go a couple of inches. Then she'd turn to the guy and they'd both giggle. It was obvious that the worse shot she took, the cuter they both thought it was.

"I might have to forfeit," the girl said between giggles.

"I might have to vomit," Beth muttered.

George tapped Beth's shoulder with his own.

"Hey, Beth, where's your sense of romance?" he whispered.

Beth rolled her eyes. "George, I have a sense of romance, but *romance* has no sense of *me*."

Beth knew that he knew it was true. She had always loved boys. As a kid, she used to chase them around the playground and try to kiss them, but they always got away. And although they appreciated how good she was at sports, boys never *really* noticed her.

That is, until ninth grade, when size C alien boobs had taken over Beth's chest. Suddenly boys were standing in line to kiss her at parties. While she didn't mind the ogling, she did think it was kind of funny that guys liked her for the one thing she felt had landed on her body by mistake. Even now, two years after the breasts had arrived, Beth still felt like the Puberty Fairy had played an unfunny trick on her.

But the hooking up never led to any serious relationships. No boy Beth really liked ever returned her affections. Beth decided her love life was best described in the lyric of a song she'd heard on a classic rock station: "Love don't love you."

"But maybe that'll change this summer," George offered.

"What do you mean?"

"I dunno. Maybe you'll find a summer boy."

"A summer boy?"

"Yeah, one of those guys your cousins hook up with." George nudged her and raised his eyebrows.

Beth and George had become friends at a party two years ago. Instead of staring at Beth's breasts, George had chatted with her about sports, school, whatever. Beth had known right off that she wasn't attracted to him — he was too skinny and pale, and she didn't go for guys with curly hair. But at the same time, she'd felt something click. She and George were platonic soul mates, like Will and Grace, only without the gay thing. They'd been inseparable ever since.

Beth eyed the couple ahead of them again. The guy had his hand on the woman's butt.

"Like that guy? Is he a summer boy?" she asked George.

George took a quick glance at him. "Could be. They look really smitten, like they haven't known each other long enough to figure out that the other person is actually going to drive them crazy. Definitely an indication of a summer thing."

"You seem to know a lot about it, George. When did you meet your summer boy?" Beth teased.

George was undeterred. "Don't you worry about me. I'll get some action this time. I'm declaring this the summer of George!"

Beth rolled her eyes. George had been saying that since he'd seen it on a *Seinfeld* rerun, and not once had any summer turned out to be his. Of course, this summer he was staying at the beach until mid-August, which allowed for more exposure than staying at home and working at the Family Dollar in Martin, Massachusetts.

"I'm telling you, Beth. Summer's the time to act. New places, new faces . . ."

His voice trailed off, and they both turned to watch the couple again.

"I'm *sooooo* bad!" The brunette was crooning, finally plunking the ball into the hole.

"You had just two strokes, right?" the guy said, grinning and writing her bogus score on his golf card. They finally moved to the next hole.

"Praise Jesus," George said. But now Beth was absorbed.

"It's hopeless, George. All guys want *that*." She nodded toward the annoying woman. "They want flirty. They want girly. I'm not either."

"What?" George asked, looking over his shoulder to follow Beth's gaze. "That?" George said loudly, pointing his club in the woman's direction. "Are you kidding?"

Beth grabbed George's club and shushed him.

"No way," he said, lowering his voice. "That annoying giggler's got nothing on you." He gave her his lopsided grin. George could be incredibly charming when he wanted to be.

"Well, it seems that way," she said, touching but not hitting her ball, just trying to get the angle that would take it home. "I mean, look at the facts. She's here hooking up and I'm here with . . . you."

"Okay, I'm going to pretend you didn't just insult me, because I must have pity for those who lose to me in minigolf," George said with a sly grin. "But seriously, Beth, you're pretty and you're fun to be around. You're gonna find your guy. It's only a matter of time."

Beth looked away quickly. She couldn't explain it, but whenever George complimented her like that, it felt weird.

"Thanks," she said nonchalantly. Finally, she took aim and hit the ball. It sailed past the curves of the trunk, one, two, three. "You know, you're pretty, too. In fact, I don't think the Fab Five would change a thing about you."

"Oh, that's really funny. Now you're doing *Queer Eye* jokes."

Then the sound of the ball clunking into the hole echoed throughout the course. It was her second hole in one of the game — she was mounting a comeback of megaproportions. Beth tried not to smile too big, but she couldn't help it. Maybe her winning minigolf was a sign that she could triumph over her sucky love life as well.

George and all other boys beware.

4

Jamie leaned back in the hammock, taking the ball of white yarn on her lap and straightening it so that the loops smoothed themselves out. She was three-quarters of the way done with the tiny hat she was knitting for her mom's schnauzer, Schmidty. Her mom had requested it, claiming that Schmidty couldn't stand the New Jersey winters. Personally, Jamie thought Schmidty wasn't bothered by the cold one way or the other. But she loved knitting, so she didn't mind humoring her mom. Anyway, it gave her something to do with her hands until Ethan came over.

The phone rang in the cottage a few yards behind her, but it stopped almost immediately, and she could tell by the sound of her aunt Claire chattering that the call wasn't for her. That was fine. *Knit, purl, knit, purl* — her fingers worked the needles deftly in flashes of silver.

It was her first full day at Pebble Beach. She guessed it wasn't so bad that Ethan had made plans to go dirt biking with his friends for a few hours, but she'd been expecting him to block out

23

the whole day — maybe even the whole week — just for her. Between the crowds at the party last night and the walk home with Ella, Beth, and George, they'd hardly had any time alone. Still, Ethan was independent and free-spirited — and she loved that about him. She didn't ever want to be one of those clingy, possessive, my-boyfriend-is-my-life-and-without-him-I'm-nothing girls.

Jamie held up the half-finished hat in the air and inspected the ear holes. She couldn't wait to show it to Ethan. He loved all the stupid little things Jamie liked to make with her hands. It was almost like she couldn't ever keep her fingers still, and he said that her creativity was sexy. Before Ethan, Jamie had never thought of herself like that.

Suddenly, Jamie heard heavy footsteps coming across the deck, and she knew it was him.

"The artist at work," Ethan said, coming up behind her and wrapping his arms around her. He nestled his chin into her neck and she dropped her knitting, curling up a bit because of the shivers that raced down her spine from being embraced by him. She turned her head and their lips met, which made Jamie feel like there was no one in the world but the two of them. He pulled back to look at her.

"Hi, gorgeous," she whispered, barely able to contain her giddiness. It still shocked Jamie that such an amazing guy thought *she* was beautiful. He had a swimmer's body — taut and toned with lean muscles. He had wavy, sand-colored hair that constantly got in his eyes — he usually brushed stray strands from his brow in an alluring way. There was just something about him that made him magnetic, and Jamie couldn't pull herself away from him, not that she even wanted to try.

Two weeks into her trip to Maine last summer, Jamie had been sitting on a beach chair with a pen and a stack of loose-leaf paper, imagining herself as an early twentieth-century novelist. She'd been trying to write a short story about seagulls, but instead, she'd ended up watching Ethan. He and some other guys were playing football in the sand, and she couldn't take her eyes off him.

Whenever he looked up at her, Jamie quickly frowned back down at her story, pretending she was deep in thought instead of checking out this guy's extremely cute butt. Then suddenly, he'd appeared beside her chair, all sweaty and glistening, and asked her what she was writing. She was sure that any moment his girlfriend would show up in her thong and they'd run off into the waves together, so what the hell. She'd told him about the seagulls. And he'd admitted that he was an aspiring writer, too.

She almost went into cardiac arrest when he'd asked her out. And now, in the hammock, he was making her heart pound again.

"Let's go for a ride down to the beach," Ethan suggested, and pulled Jamie up beside him.

They went into the cottage shed and dug out the black eighteen-speed Lemonde Jamie had ridden last summer, before she'd gotten her license. Ethan's own bike was muddy from wherever he'd been that morning. He took off in front of her, and Jamie pedaled as fast as she could to keep up, the wind blowing through her hair. Being in love and outside and moving fast made her feel like her body was too small for the surge of emotions that were swirling around inside her. They hurtled along the dirt path and then out onto the main road in town, Ethan leading the way. He finally slowed down alongside the pier, hopping off his bike and leaning it against a lamppost. Hand in hand, they trudged to the dunes farther up the beach and collapsed in exhaustion.

"I can't believe we have the whole summer," Jamie said through quick inhales and exhales. The blue sky they were staring at was perfectly clear.

"Yeah. There's so much going on — it's gonna be crazy." Ethan rubbed his chin excitedly. "Did I tell you I enrolled in a writing course at U. Penn this August?"

"No," she said frowning. "How long will you be gone?" Ethan lived in Philadelphia, which now seemed so far away. He tugged the strap of her green vintage halter top, the one he'd liked so much last summer. There was some kind of live wire in her chest, and it zinged whenever he touched her.

"Two weeks, from the eighth through twenty-second. I won't be coming back afterwards," he answered.

"You're going away two weeks early?" Jamie sat up and stared at him, trying to suppress the disjointed, hurt feeling that erupted deep in her gut. Ethan slipped an arm around her waist and pulled her close with an amused smile.

"Don't worry. We'll make up for the lost time," he said. He studied her intently. "Do you know how pretty you are? You have the coolest cat eyes."

Jamie still wasn't able to stop frowning. A part of her knew that it wasn't a big deal — this class seemed like an amazing opportunity, and had *she* been given the chance to go, she might have taken it, just like Ethan had. What bothered her was that he didn't seemed concerned at all that they were going to have two fewer weeks to be with each other. Hadn't their year apart made any difference to him at all?

"Well, aren't you going to miss me when you go?" After Jamie said that, she wanted to take it all back. Remarks like that were reserved for clingy girlfriends, and that was definitely something Jamie *didn't* want to be.

Ethan sighed and his mouth settled into a straight line. He didn't respond.

"I'm sorry, I didn't mean anything by that. It's just that I thought you'd want us to be . . . together . . . ," Jamie said timidly. Suddenly, she was feeling incredibly insecure.

Ethan tilted his chin away from her, staring off into nothing. He took a couple of deep breaths and then shook his head. Jamie tucked her knees up to her chin and hugged them. Then Ethan faced her again.

"Hey," he said as he stroked her bare arm with one finger. "Looks like your sunburn healed okay." He tugged at her halter strap again.

Jamie giggled a little bit at Ethan's teasing comment. Last year she'd forgotten to use sunblock during her final week at the beach, and her fairer-than-fair skin had turned lobster-red, keeping her indoors for the last days of the summer. Her only consolation had been Ethan. While everyone was outdoors swimming and barbecuing, Ethan (who could sit in the sun wearing nothing but SPF 2 and never get burned) sat with his feet propped on the bed reading *Slaughterhouse Five* to her, and rubbing cold aloe from the fridge on her arms and legs whenever she asked. Jamie had loved the attention, even though she had been all raw and red. She'd had Ethan all to herself, which was what she'd wanted all summer, anyway.

On the second afternoon, he'd gently slipped her shirt off over her head while she was lying on her stomach, and started kissing all the parts that hurt. Everyone else was down at the beach. Though it had been sweaty and sticky-hot, he'd pulled a sheet over them and traced her bare skin with his hands, which were twice as big as her own. She rolled over and touched the parts of him that fascinated her — his chest, his arms, the crease in his lower back. Then, before she knew it, he reached down and pulled off his boxers. She felt shy for a moment, but then she let him slide her own underwear down. And when they started kissing, she didn't feel shy anymore. It was thoughtful, slow, and perhaps even a little less passionate than Jamie had expected. It all happened so naturally somehow. Still, more important, when it was over, it felt right. She'd been attracted to Ethan up to then, but that was the moment when she'd felt her life tying up with his in a knot. It was the first time she had felt — dare she say it — like she was falling in love.

"Those were some good times, huh?" Ethan said, kissing her shoulder. The kiss made her pulse quicken and her heart fill up with sheer joy. She lifted her finger up to the scar on Ethan's chin, which he'd gotten years ago while riding his bike. Then she ran her hands over his stubble-covered cheeks.

"Yes, they were," she replied softly.

The light had changed within the past few minutes, and the sounds of the waves became somewhat muted and distant. Dusk was Jamie's favorite time of day. All the colors in the sky transformed from wondrous hues of blues into shades of red and violet. She slid a hand under Ethan's T-shirt and ran her fingers over where his boxers covered his left hip bone. This subtle spot was one of her favorite parts of his body—she couldn't get over how perfectly sculptured he was. But her attraction to him wasn't just physical. She had the same feeling now that she had that day they spent under the sheets. She wanted him to see her soul in her eyes and know that it was meant to be.

She wanted this to last forever. There was no reason why it shouldn't.

But their earlier tiff had left a bit of awkwardness in the air between them, and it wasn't so easy to send away. It lingered in the back of her mind until she let herself be swept away by the sight of the sunset. Then when Ethan turned to kiss her again, she stopped thinking about anything at all.

5

Ella sat at the picnic table by the grill, her chin in her hands so that her full, freshly glossed lips smushed against her palms. She was chewing her fifth stick of gum of the day and watching backyard badminton. It was Team Peter and Kelsi versus Team Beth and George. Although it was a fair match, George and Beth were winning, mostly because Peter was clearly distracted. Whenever Kelsi took a swing with her racket, he followed every motion of her body as if she were Anna Kournikova.

Ella tried to take her mind off her envy and put it toward better use — checking out Peter's amazing body. He was wearing aqua-blue shorts and a tank top that had the word PUNK across the front. His tan arms were a little sweaty from the heat of the competition. She admired his athletic build, big calves, and the strong muscles in his back that flexed whenever he moved his arms an inch. He walked in a slow, deliberate way that just drove Ella wild. The smoothness of each one of his strides gave off this air of confidence that Ella had always felt in herself, but never really saw in anyone else. Every two seconds, Ella was thinking about what he might look like underneath his clothes. She couldn't help herself.

Up until he'd walked into the backyard about half an hour ago, the hottie singer from the party had almost become a memory to Ella. He hadn't called Kelsi until this morning. And Ella hadn't seen him for over a week, so she'd lost hold of the thing that had made him so irresistible to her that first night.

Now it was all coming back to her.

Ella reached for the tie of her leopard-pattern bikini top and readjusted the knot. She found herself wondering how she looked, which she usually never worried about. She wished Peter had come down to the beach earlier, when she had been lying on her stomach in her tiny bikini bottom, the back of her top untied and open. That might have convinced him to grease her up with Coppertone instead of seeking out Kelsi.

"Good one," Kelsi said, bending over to pick up a birdie that George had spiked hard against the ground. Peter playfully patted her on the butt as she bent over. She shot up awkwardly, her short blonde ponytail swinging, and darted a look toward the grown-ups. Beth's dad was bent over the grill, laying raw pink burgers on the grate. Uncle Carr and Aunt Claire, Beth's mom, and Ella and Kelsi's dad — their parents were divorced, so the sisters spent the summers with their father — were at the table across the grass, too busy chatting to notice the innocent hanky-panky between Peter and Kelsi.

Kelsi was always uptight and conservative when it came to public displays of affection. Ella chuckled at her sister's prudish reaction. If Peter thought Kelsi was *that* kind of girl — the kind that let you touch her butt — he was sorely mistaken. Big sis had gone out with her last boyfriend for two years and only let him get to third base. *Two years.* For Kelsi, who lived by the mantra "Let's slow down," the standard allowable butt-touching time was probably somewhere around six months. Ella, on the other hand, didn't have those kinds of strict rules. In fact, she considered all rules to be rather flexible, especially if they interfered with having fun. And when it came to Peter, any and all types of restrictions or regulations could be easily thrown out the window.

"Get ready, guys. The best burgers in the history of ground beef are about to be served," Gary, Beth's dad, pronounced from behind the grill. They had burgers at least three times a week at these cookouts, but Gary always got excited about it. And so did George, who was a big fan of Gary's burgers. George abandoned the badminton game and leaned over the grill to watch Gary work.

"You know, these things are cooking too slow, Gar," he said. "You need some of this action." Before anyone could figure out what he was doing, he picked up the lighter fluid beside the grill and squirted some into the coals. A huge flame leaped up. Everyone, including Ella, jumped back in fear.

Beth stood behind George, shaking her head sympathetically at her dad.

"George, kindly step away from the grill," Gary said, swiping at his face to make sure it was still there. "And while you're at it, don't handle anything flammable ever again. Okay, buddy?"

George's face flooded bright red. Uncle Gary began scraping the burgers off the grate onto a platter, then disappeared inside. Kelsi immediately stepped in to take over with the survivors, expertly sliding the spatula under each raw patty, one at a time.

Ella couldn't help but laugh. She just loved a commotion. She turned to look at Peter, who stood aimlessly between the grill and the net. He slouched on one hip and cast his gaze over the grass slowly. He was trying hard to conceal a huge grin, which Ella imagined was directed at the near-fatal barbecue. The fact that they were the only two people laughing made her feel as if they were in on some private joke that nobody else was a part of. It was like a sign that Ella couldn't ignore. She just had to make a move.

As she stood up and sauntered toward him, she adjusted her top to show a little more skin.

"You up for a game of one-on-one?" she asked, boldly grabbing one of the two badminton rackets dangling from Peter's hands and started back toward the net.

"Is that some sort of challenge?" he asked, glancing back at Kelsi.

"For you, maybe. I'm a badminton expert."

She wasn't lying. After years of coming to Pebble Beach, badminton had become her sport (if you could even call it that). And besides, she looked good playing it. She was wearing a tiny white FCUK tennis skirt below her bikini top to show off her newly tanned arms, legs, and stomach.

Knowing how delicate boys' egos could be, she intentionally missed the birdie on Peter's first serve. She laughed and bent to pick it up, giving him a close-up view of her backside before handing over the birdie to him.

"Lucky serve," she said slyly while arching one eyebrow.

"Are you kidding? That was one hundred percent pure skill," he replied. His eyes met Ella's for a second with the slight yet oh-dear-God-how-sexy smile still playing on his lips. She tried not to be rendered to pure mush at the sight of it.

As long as she'd been noticing boys, Ella had known she could cast a spell on them if she wanted. All she had to do to get a guy to like her was focus completely on him, and soon he would be under her control. But Peter was proving to be something of a challenge.

The next time he served, she missed completely by accident, and the birdie sailed right past her.

"Expert, did you say? You're a badminton expert?" Peter asked teasingly.

"Listen, I just didn't want to take away your dignity so quickly," Ella said through her giggles. "But now that you're mocking me, I'll just have to whip you."

They snapped back and forth, both getting more and more competitive. Toward the end of the match, with Ella up by a couple of points, the birdie landed on the edge of some trees and Ella ran over to retrieve it. Her heart was thrumming. Beating the brush with her fingers, she grasped the birdie and stood up, turning around with her racket poised to serve, her cheeks flushed. Only Peter wasn't waiting for her eagerly, as she had hoped. His racket was on the grass underneath the net.

Ella looked toward the grill and saw that he was standing behind Kelsi, holding out a plate for the new batch of burgers. Every time she passed a burger to Peter, Kelsi's entire face lit up like a Christmas tree.

Across the lawn, Ella swiped at the perspiration on her cheeks. She was still trying to regain her breath. She hadn't noticed before how giddy her sister looked when Peter was close by. It was unbelievable but undeniable. She looked the same way Ella had *felt* a few seconds before, when she and Peter were volleying back and forth.

She looked like a girl who was falling in love.

Ella forced herself to accept the situation. Kelsi was her sister. And for some reason that Ella couldn't even begin to imagine, Peter seemed really into Kelsi. The smart thing for Ella to do would be to forget him for good and move on to the next summer boy.

But it wouldn't be the easiest thing to do.

Jamie paused by the side of Ethan's house and pulled off her cotton sun hat, smoothing back her damp hair. She resecured the knotty bun she'd made before leaving her house as she walked up the stairs, then lowered her hand and pushed the doorbell with her index finger. Her breath fluttered out of her mouth unevenly while she waited.

Underneath her loose peasant blouse she wore the pink sheer bra that she'd bought over the winter with Ethan in mind. He hadn't seen her wear it before, so today would be the grand unveiling. She wondered what his reaction would be — would he pounce on her and smother her with kisses, or would he just say she looked pretty and then act all weird? With Ethan lately, you could never quite tell what mood he was going to be in — either he was attentive and affectionate or distant and standoffish. They hadn't even had sex again. Jamie was beginning to worry.

The past two-and-a-half weeks hadn't been quite what Jamie had expected in the days leading up to the summer. She'd pictured her and Ethan spending long hours lying on the beach, cuddling and kissing, and drinking iced coffees at local cafés. But so far, he'd been busy a lot of the time at his job down at Pebble Beach Bikes, or with his friends doing typical guy stuff like fooling around with the X-Box for hours on end.

But today is going to be different, Jamie kept telling herself. They hadn't been together — as in, alone in a house with a bed — since she'd gotten here. And that was all going to change as soon as Ethan opened the door.

The doorknob jiggled and Jamie tried to let her body relax, rolling her shoulders back a few times to relieve the tension.

Ethan's mother appeared in the doorway.

"Oh," Jamie said in surprise. "Hi there."

Mrs. Davis was a tall, statuesque woman with a short brunette bob that made her look very first lady-ish, even in a swimsuit and flip-flops, which she wore now. She gave Jamie a friendly smile and welcomed her inside.

"Jamie, so nice to see you," she said. "I was just leaving for the beach. Ethan's downstairs. They're watching a movie."

"Great. Thanks."

Jamie turned and headed down the stairs. She could hear the movie blaring from the VCR. Definitely *Star Wars*. It was Ethan's favorite. Yoda was giving Luke Skywalker his famous speech about how you couldn't try to use the force, you just had to *do* it. "Do, or do not. There is no try."

Maybe she'd come over too early. She knew Ethan usually liked to lie on the couch and watch TV in the morning. But as she ducked under the archway into the den, she saw four of Ethan's friends, crashed out on the white leather sofa and chairs. He was in the chair on the far end, his legs hanging over the side, his hair all crooked and smushed from lying around. He looked up just as she entered the room.

"Hey," he said, frowning slightly.

"Hi." Jamie walked around behind the couch and kissed him on the cheek. "What's up?"

"Nothing. What are you doing here?"

Jamie looked around the room at the other guys. One of them sat up, grabbed the remote from the coffee table, and paused the movie. Were they having some kind of guys-only thing? Her chest pinched a little as she looked back at Ethan.

"I just thought, well, last time we talked you said we'd have the house to ourselves," Jamie said very softly so that Ethan's friends wouldn't hear her. Had she done something wrong? She racked her brain but she couldn't think of anything.

She looked around the room again, wishing that the other boys would just vanish into thin air. That way, she could tell Ethan how much she longed to be next to him, how she desperately needed to have that feeling she experienced last summer — like their souls fit perfectly together. But Ethan's friends didn't look like they were going anywhere. In fact, it appeared to her that she might be the one on the way out.

"I just, you know, missed you," she muttered again, low enough for only Ethan to hear. She gave him a tender smile, but he kept looking at his watch and glancing at the TV set.

Okay, she told herself, *it's a guy thing. Shouldn't take this personally at all.* But she could barely contain the tears that were welling up in her eyes.

"Well, I guess I should go," Jamie said, trying not to lose her composure. She would never be able to forgive herself for breaking down in front of Ethan and his posse. But before she could say anything else, Ethan did something nice. He made her feel like a part of the gang.

"Hey, you haven't met these guys yet, right? These are some of my best buddies." Ethan waved a hand over his three friends. "Scott, Alex, Keith . . . this is my Jamie."

My Jamie? Ethan had momentarily redeemed himself.

"Have a seat," Scott said as he cleared a spot for her beside him on the couch. His foot grazed the miniature Millennium Falcon replica perched on the table.

"Careful," Ethan said, leaning forward protectively. He'd built the model from an elaborate vintage kit last year. Jamie knew it was his one nerdy hobby, and that all his friends made fun of him for it. But she'd always thought the patience it must have taken was something else to love about him.

Finally, everyone was situated. "So, I hear you're a writer, Jamie," Scott said, ignoring the fact that the movie was still on pause. Scott was classic surfer guy material. His hair was brown and fuzzy, and he had wide-set hazel eyes. Jamie's first thought was to introduce him to Ella — he was definitely cute enough.

"Aspiring," she said humbly. She never liked talking about her writing with anyone except Ethan. "What about you?" She quickly checked on Ethan, who'd started the movie again on a low volume.

"Well, I'm not an aspiring anything," he said. "I help my dad. He runs a business flying planes, you know the ones with the ads that fly over the beach?"

Jamie nodded, although she wasn't really listening. Her thoughts were on Ethan and whether or not she had been giving him enough space over the past couple of weeks after all. Yesterday she'd dragged him to the beach and talked to him nonstop while he barely said a word. Sometimes she just couldn't help herself — Ethan made her feel so comfortable that she oftentimes confided in him about things she had kept hidden from everyone else. But maybe that was too overwhelming for him.

Eventually, Scott stopped talking and Jamie's attention returned to her surroundings. While everyone focused on the movie again, Jamie studied the Millennium Falcon, partly because it was blocking her view, but mostly because it never failed to impress her. It was such an elaborate piece of craftsmanship. She just couldn't believe that Ethan was responsible for its creation.

Jamie stayed for the rest of the movie. When it was over, the boys remained seated. Jamie stood up and stretched her arms above her head as if she had been sitting down for days. It seemed she wasn't going to get any private time with Ethan, so she decided to head out.

"Well, guys, I have some stuff to do, so I'll catch you later," she said.

"James, it's been real," Scott said and shot her a surfer hang-ten sign with his right hand.

"Absolutely," she replied with an equally corny thumbs-up.

Ethan stood up and walked her to the downstairs door, which led onto the back deck that faced the ocean.

"Hey, thanks for not kicking me out earlier," she said, trying to sound breezy and carefree.

"Sorry about the misunderstanding," he replied, his hands in his pockets.

"Yeah, well, it happens," Jamie said sweetly. She gave Ethan a peck on the cheek and walked onto the deck.

She wasn't codependent or anything like that, she told herself. Maybe she'd go home and write, or draw, or swim. There were plenty of things she was happy to do alone.

But before she did, there was one thing she had to accomplish.

Without even really thinking about what she was about to do, she spun around.

"Hey, Ethan!" she called out. He turned around rather quickly as if she had startled him.

"Just wanted you to see what you missed," she said.

She lifted up her peasant blouse and quickly flashed him the pink bra. His eyes widened and his jaw dropped. Jamie lowered her shirt, waved, and walked off, happy that she hadn't let him see her cry.

What Beth liked about the houses along Peachtree Road, other than that they were practically right on the beach, was that they were multicolored — soft pink, soft turquoise, white, beige, red. In the midday sun, the paints reflected even brighter, and to Beth, they looked like Fruity Pebbles.

"C'mon, George," she called over her shoulder. He was straggling with the family's lone surfboard, carrying it carefully, slowly picking his way along the road in his bare feet.

"I told you to wear sandals. I don't know why you didn't listen to me," Beth reprimanded him sternly. George was on what he called a "personal journey," meaning he was trying to achieve spiritual enlightenment by not wearing shoes for the entire summer. He'd gotten it from some friend who was into Buddhism.

"I'm fine. And stop talking to me like you're my mother. It's creepy. And annoying!" George said, hefting the board tighter under his arm. But Beth knew the pavement was hot and the soles of

George's feet were definitely burning up. She couldn't help but chuckle.

"Speaking of your mom, what did she have to say when she called last night?" Beth asked.

"She said she doesn't miss me." He used his free arm to shoo a seagull that flew by him. "And she said she's glad to know I have *you* to watch over me." He smiled wryly.

Within minutes, George was several paces ahead. He was engaged in some sort of weird jog, lifting his feet in stiff little jerks and hurrying toward the grass that led to the beach. "Great balls of fire," he exclaimed after he threw the board over his shoulder. Beth snorted as she followed him over the curb.

Up ahead, the Tuttles had set up camp in their usual spot. An orange umbrella announced their location, and the adults were clustered beneath it. Beth could see Kelsi and her new boyfriend playing Frisbee, and Ella lying on her towel. Not far from Ella a girl reclined on a lounge chair under an identical orange umbrella. Beth always thought lounge chairs and umbrellas were for wusses. For her, there was nothing better than splaying out on good old-fashioned sand smack dab in the middle of harmful UV rays.

She plopped herself down next to Ella, and George collapsed onto his knees on her left. He checked out the lounge chair girl for a few seconds (in the cursory way he checked out every girl) and then lay down on his stomach. He and Beth looked at each other with their cheeks pressed up against their forearms.

"Gotta get nice and hot first," George said, which was exactly what Beth was thinking. There was a right way and a wrong way to enter the ocean, and the right way was after your body temperature reached a full-on I'm-as-roasted-as-a-Planters-peanut type of hot.

Suddenly, George lifted his head to look at the girl on the lounge chair, his chin on his knuckles. She was drinking a Diet Vanilla Coke, tilting her head back and gulping deeply, looking suspiciously like an advertisement.

"God, that's enough to make a man switch to Diet Coke," George murmured.

She was wearing a low-cut red bathing suit and two clips in her long, reddish-brown hair, '40s retro style. Beth had to admit, this girl was working it big-time.

"I have an extra one. Do you want it?" the sexy siren asked George, without noticing the suggestiveness of what she just said.

Beth and George both stared blankly at the girl. Did she have supersonic hearing? Or ESP? She leaned forward in her chair and pulled her sunglasses off. "Really, it's getting warm, anyway."

"I love warm soda," George said, watching the girl as she rose from her seat and walked toward them. She knelt beside them and handed George the extra can of Diet Coke, then folded her hands over her knees.

"Do you guys surf?" She nodded her head at the surfboard.

"A little. We're not great or anything," Beth replied.

Last spring, she and George had rented *Blue Crush* and ended up watching it four times in one weekend. They'd lain on George's bed eating chips and drinking root beer and ended up with a pukey, dazed feeling that George later called "The Sickness." When George had come to Maine last year, they'd taken surfing lessons as a tribute to the event.

"Personally, I'm pretty much a pro," George said sarcastically.

The girl nodded, not seeming to get the joke. "I'd love to learn."

"Really?" Beth studied the girl's small frame, her perfect posture, and the way her hands were folded on her lap. This girl was not surfing material.

"Yeah. But I'm not supposed to because I might damage my hands."

George and Beth both surveyed her hands at the same instant.

"What's so great about your hands?" George asked honestly.

"Oh well, it's not that my hands are great. It's just that I play the violin, so breaking a wrist bone or something like that wouldn't be such a good idea." The girl ran her fingers through her long, straight, copper hair for emphasis, and adjusted a hair clip. Beth's immediate thought was that nobody wants to break bones. Were violin hands *really* more important than everyone else's?

"So, the violin, huh?" George was always a master conversationalist.

"Yeah, I'm in the music program at NYU." Beth noted that the girl said it with a certain amount of pride and perfect diction.

"I'm Cara, by the way," she said and reached out her hand formally. Beth shook it lightly.

"I'm Beth."

"And I'm George. Such a pleasure to meet you," he said as he dipped in a mock bow. Clearly, Cara thought he was funny because Beth never saw a girl laugh so hard. At George in a mean way, yes. At George in a flirty way, never.

"Are you good at it?" he asked.

Cara shrugged with a modest smile. "I hope. Supposedly my teacher thinks I have a lot of potential."

45

"Wow," Beth said, fairly impressed. Everyone said she had potential in athletics. But that didn't seem as complex and intriguing as being a promising violinist.

George had turned to stare off longingly at the water.

"Why don't you go in first, George?" Beth asked, nodding toward the surfboard.

Before she'd finished the sentence, he was up and pulling off his shirt, revealing his smooth, freckled chest.

"Later, dudettes." George grabbed the surfboard and headed toward the ocean. Beth watched him trot down to the water. The backs of his legs were dusted with sand. George always looked funny carrying a surfboard — it always seemed way too big for him.

"How long have you guys been dating?" Cara asked Beth after a moment

"We're not dating." Beth noticed an ant crawling on her arm. She blew at it and it went flying off into the air. "We're just friends."

"Oh?" Cara looked surprised. "Really?"

"Yep. We've been for quite a while now."

"Don't you think he's cute?"

Beth scrunched up her forehead at Cara. "You think?"

"Yes, without a doubt." They both stared out at the water to determine who was right about George. Beth had never heard anybody describe him as cute before. Goofy, definitely. But cute? That was a first.

George was waist-deep in water and waiting for a wave. When one came, he crawled up onto his board. As he stood on the surfboard, his body moved smoothly. His feet were planted firmly but the rest of him was moving fluidly to balance himself. In another second, the board descended and he fell forward into the water.

Beth had to admit, when George wasn't on land, he did have a certain grace. His curly dark head disappeared underwater and popped up again, and he blew some water out of his mouth and swiped his free hand at his face. Okay, maybe he was a small touch of cute.

Beth then stole a glance at Cara, who still had her eyes on George. She had glossy, penny-colored hair and those deep brown eyes. Beth felt like she had been cast under a dark shadow all of a sudden.

"Really cute," Cara repeated herself and then sipped some more of her Coke. "Is he single?"

The question made something in Beth go haywire. There was a burning sensation in her chest. And her skin started to feel real itchy for some reason. She wanted to stop this conversation and head home to recover from this visitation of "The Sickness II," but all she could do was smile and reply.

"Yes, he's as available as they come."

When George came back, he stood over Beth, one foot on either side of her waist, his cold ankles pressing against her thighs. He shook himself off, the water hitting her in fast droplets.

She grabbed his ankle to stop him, digging her nails gently into his skin. "Damn it, George."

"Your turn," he said, plopping down beside her and panting, not caring that he was covering himself with sand and her with water. His hair stood up in spikes. Beth smoothed them out for him with a swipe, then stood up and grabbed the board.

Out in the water, Beth took several deep breaths. She just loved the feeling of her lungs expanding. The water was cold. It was still June, and it hadn't been hot enough for it to really warm up. She walked in up to her thighs and then dunked herself entirely. She jumped up and whipped her wet hair back from her face.

She crawled up on the board and paddled out much farther than George had. She didn't want to be near any of the other swimmers — they always made her feel a bit more nervous when she was on the board, since she had to keep her eyes peeled to make sure that she didn't topple over onto anyone if she wiped out. Beth treaded water while she waited for a wave to come. She felt a slight uneasiness in her stomach again, and she couldn't figure out why. Okay, she did know why. She didn't like Cara. There was something about her that just made Beth queasy. It was strange because Beth usually liked everyone.

Every once in a while, a minor ripple passed her, and she'd bob up and down rhythmically. Beth felt truly happy out in the ocean. She liked to feel her body at work as her own strength kept her afloat. When a wave swelled twenty yards away, she turned so that her back faced it and waited. Beth thought the waiting was almost as good as the surfing — the anticipation was a big part of the adrenaline rush. She waited to see how big the wave would get, waited for the little pinch of fear that came while she watched. Finally, it was just behind her, and Beth climbed onto the board, stood up, and glided.

When she trudged back onto shore about half an hour later, her legs and arms felt like marshmallows. She breathed heavily as she hoisted the board up and made her way across the sand, her feet sinking into thousands of tiny grains at every step, which made it very hard to walk without stumbling around like a toddler. When she got to the group of Tuttles, she sat down hard, pulled in her legs Indian style and leaned back on the palms of her hands.

George had his legs near Cara's, his toes almost touching her thigh. He flung his head back on his neck to look up at Beth. "So, how was it? Like a scene out of *Blue Crush,* right?"

"Good, but not *that* good," she said through short-winded gasps. For some reason, she couldn't take her eyes off the spot where George's feet and Cara's thigh were nearly touching. "Did you see that last one?" The wave had been enormous. She had been just about to give up and come in when it had barreled up behind her. But Beth hung in there and took it on like a pro.

"Nah," George shook his head remorsefully. "We were talking about . . . what were we talking about?" He lowered his chin back to Cara.

"Doing shots."

"Right. Butterscotch shots. Cara says she's never had one. And I think we should get that remedied sometime soon. Before she gets all shriveled and old and it's too late."

Cara giggled. "You can buy me one later."

"You can buy *me* one later," George said.

Beth watched as George poked at Cara's arm. *Oh . . . my . . . . God,* she thought to herself. *They are flirting!*

It was just too much for her to handle — George and flirting and Cara and sun and waves and George again. Yes, she had to get out of there right away or she might suddenly combust from all the stress.

"Well, I'm gonna head home and shower," Beth said, standing

up and brushing herself off like a first-rate obsessive-compulsive. She was still wet, so no matter how much she kept trying to brush the sand away, it stuck to her arms and legs and white swimsuit like Krazy Glue. Nevertheless, she wouldn't stop until each granule of the beach was wiped off her skin. Actually, she was acting so hyper, one might say she was turning into George.

Which may have been why George hopped up and came to the rescue.

"Yeah, I'm going to bail, too," he said, handing Beth a towel. "Here, this might help you get the sand off."

Beth managed to sweep all the sand to the ground and then wrapped the towel around her waist.

"George, it's fine if you want to stay," Beth said in an indifferent tone. This was so weird. Suddenly, she was painfully aware that she wanted him to come in spite of what she had said.

George hesitated for a moment and eyed Beth thoughtfully. "C'mon, you know you can't live without me."

Beth rolled her eyes before waving awkwardly to Cara and then headed back to the house in the direction they'd come. George came up from behind with the surfboard, and she helped him out by holding up the front.

At the edge of the beach, where they had to step over the curb, George put down his end of the board to get a better grip, and as he stood up again, he peered back over his shoulder. Cara was still visible near her orange umbrella. She was taking a swig of her Diet Vanilla Coke, but she stopped suddenly and waved at them.

"She's cute, don't you think?" George asked, picking up the board again. Beth couldn't bring herself to say anything.

"Wouldn't give me the time of day, right?" he asked again, turning back toward her, resigned, but content.

Beth just kept staring off into space. She couldn't get an insane image out of her mind: George running up on the beach in perfect *Baywatch*-style super-slow motion.

"Hello in there," George said as he tapped lightly on Beth's forehead. "Anyone home? Jesus, Beth. You're a million miles away."

"Yeah, uh. Sorry about that. I was just thinking. . . ."

About what Cara had said about him being cute, about her selfish feelings that told her that George — in a totally platonic way, of course — was hers. That it might turn out to be the summer of George, after all.

8

The Tuttles did so much barbecuing that, on the Fourth of July, they celebrated by *not* barbecuing.

Ella spent the whole morning in her strapless polka-dot bikini, snoozing on the hammock in the backyard and drinking some iced tea that she'd spiked with Jack Daniel's from her dad's liquor cabinet. She was deliberately avoiding her favorite glossy fashion mags, and had plucked a couple of *National Geographic*s out of the pile by Kelsi's bed earlier that morning. Whenever she thumbed through Kelsi's more intellectual reading material, she thought about the nuns at her school in New Canaan, Connecticut, and wondered what it would be like if they fussed over her the way they did over Kelsi, instead of yelling at her for passing notes and sneaking out at lunch. But somewhere in between the photos of African villagers and the articles on the preservation of the rain forest, Ella's mind started to wander, and suddenly she was fantasizing about being profiled on E! because of her stellar fashion sense.

It was swelteringly hot and humid outside. There wasn't a cloud in the sky, and the sun felt so strong that Ella kept picking up the glass of iced tea she'd lodged into the grass and holding it against the outside of her thighs in order to cool off.

She was considering packing up her things and running into the kitchen for a snack when the screen door slid open and Kelsi and Peter stepped onto the deck.

On second thought, maybe I'll stay put, Ella thought to herself as she put a piece of gum in her mouth and started chomping on it furiously. She could see out of the corner of her eye that they were at the table under the umbrella, holding hands like a honeymooning couple.

Ella let out a frustrated sigh, slammed the magazine shut, and dropped it onto the grass. She then picked up a copy of *Glamour* instead. She browsed through the table of contents and flipped to the makeover section, which was her personal favorite. A heavy girl with caterpillars for eyebrows had gotten a pluck and color, and her cheeks and eyes had been brushed with the same flattering shade of peach. A brunette with a bad perm had had her hair straightened, and they'd penciled her lips into a pouty bow. Ella absolutely loved success stories, especially those involving makeup and hairspray.

She turned over again and put down the iced tea. She rubbed at the sweat collecting above her naturally full lips. She glanced from below lowered eyelids at Kelsi and Peter on the deck, and wondered what they were talking about.

Finally, unable to resist anymore, she rolled out of the hammock and got ready to stage a little interruption. Ella rubbed at the places where the ropes had left indentations in her skin and tugged at her swimsuit to make sure it was properly aligned. Then she padded across the grass toward the deck. An invigorating breeze came off the ocean and made her feel refreshed and alert, like she'd just had a shot of Red Bull instead of J.D.

"Hey, guys. What's going on?" Ella asked as she slipped her fingers into the waistband of her bikini bottom, snapping the elastic a little. She was trying to send out a message to Peter via mental telepathy. *Notice me.*

"We're just talking about what to do tonight," Peter answered. "Do you feel like going downtown? We can watch the fireworks from there." He met her eyes in the completely normal way people do when they ask you a simple question, like "How was your day?" or "Can you tell me where the bathroom is?" But regardless of whatever Peter had just said, Ella couldn't help but shiver as if the temperature were thirty degrees below zero.

Her body responded before her mind did, so she just nodded her head. Then suddenly her brain caught up. If they went out and partied downtown, she'd probably meet some boys. And maybe if she met a boy she liked, she could start thinking about *him* all the time instead of lusting after her older sister's boyfriend. Problem solved. It was that simple.

Now all she had to do was find something amazing to wear.

9

Jamie fiddled with her beaded necklace, refusing to look at the clock. She reached down to the hem of her denim skirt and gave it a tug. Ethan was fifteen minutes late.

The cousins and George had gone downtown to eat dinner and hang out and maybe watch the fireworks. The adults were all over at Beth's parents' place, along with the little kids. There was a warm breeze coming through the screen door that made her think about that romantic late-night picnic that she and Ethan shared on the beach last Fourth of July. Where on earth was he? If she had to wait another fifteen *seconds,* she might explode.

Instead of getting up and checking herself out in the mirror for the twentieth time, Jamie picked up one of the dusty children's books that were a permanent fixture in the cottage. *The Princess and the Pea.* She thumbed through the pages and tried to distract herself. Maybe she'd find some ideas for her own writing. Sometimes the magical kingdoms and fantastic characters in children's books really inspired her.

She was looking at an illustration of the princess lying on her enormous pile of mattresses when the screen door squeaked open. Ethan appeared in the doorway just as she stood up. He was wearing an electric blue surfing T-shirt that proclaimed HAVE A WHALE OF A DAY, and a weak smile.

The smile made Jamie feel slightly nervous.

She walked up to him, slipped her hand into his, and stood on tiptoe to kiss the corner of his lips. "Hey, good lookin'. What's up?"

He gave her a mild shrug while his hand stiffened in her grasp. "Nothing. What's up with you?"

"Not much." Had they just met or something? Jamie felt like introducing herself. *Hi, my name's Jamie. I'm your girlfriend.*

They moved over to the couch and sat down. There was nothing between them but silence.

"Are you okay?" She put her hand on his thigh.

"Yeah," he said indifferently while he aimed his gaze at the armrest of the couch.

"Good," Jamie said confidently, although she knew in her gut it wasn't true. "We have the house to ourselves," she whispered as she leaned in closer to him and grinned. Ethan, on the other hand, didn't budge or soften to her touch like he usually did.

"Jamie, I think . . ." He stopped himself so that he could swallow hard.

Okay, this is it, Jamie said to herself. Something big had gone wrong along the way. Ethan had been acting strange for weeks. She suddenly didn't want to know what it was.

"I think, maybe, you got the wrong idea," he said.

Jamie's hand fluttered to her necklace. She held her hand there for a few seconds and reminded herself to keep breathing or else she'd faint from a lack of oxygen to the brain. She cleared her throat. "Wrong idea? About what?"

"J, I think you're an amazing girl."

Oh, shit.

"I just . . . it seems like you think . . ." He took a breath. "Ever since we slept together last summer, I feel like things have been a little intense for me."

Jamie was hanging on his every word, hoping that he wasn't going to do what she expected him to.

"I had an awesome time with you last summer. I still want to hang out with you. But it's, like, you think we're more than we are. We're just enjoying each other, you know? Nothing serious."

"Nothing serious."

"I mean, I'm not, like, your boyfriend or anything. I thought things between us were more, you know, casual."

Jamie felt like her pounding heart had just collapsed into her abdomen. Not her boyfriend. Not her boyfriend.

All of a sudden, she laughed in that way someone laughs when nothing's really funny but they're too nervous to keep quiet. If only this conversation were a train and she could pull the emergency stop and escape. But then she started to think of all the reasons he *was* her boyfriend. They had spent so much time together, and she had thought they had something special.

"Ethan, this is ridiculous. We e-mailed all last year. We . . . we were *together*." Jamie said through slightly gritted teeth.

Her whole body felt like it was on fire with embarrassment and anger. She looked down at her nails and started picking at them. The fury inside of her was about to explode, and she had to calm down before it did. She was torn between feeling like she wanted to reassure him that she loved him and feeling like she wanted run him over with his precious bike. She was just so confused that all she could do was sit there and let a couple of tears stream down her flushed cheeks. There was no way to fight them back this time.

"Jamie," he said, taking a moment to wipe those tears away with his fingers. "I am so, so flattered that you like me this much. Come here." She let him pull her into a hug. "We can still hang out. Maybe we should just be friends, that's all."

Jamie pressed her face into the fabric of his T-shirt where he was holding her. She put her arms around him and squeezed very tightly. He had said *friends* — the dreaded "f" word! How could this be happening?

Ethan pulled back and lifted her chin. He kissed her cheeks, then worked his way over to her lips. Jamie could hear his breathing quicken along with the rhythm of waves crashing onto the beach. The crickets were loud tonight, too, making chirping noises as they hid up in the maple trees planted along the property line. She breathed in his kiss.

Jaime couldn't help but wonder if Ethan kissed all his friends like this. If that were true, maybe being friends wouldn't be so bad.

"We could go into my room," she blurted out, without thinking too much about how Ethan might react. She couldn't stop herself. He was so sexy. And, for some reason, he now seemed hotter than ever.

Ethan looked at her long and hard, then turned away from her. Jamie could see regret in his eyes, but she wasn't sure if he regretted breaking up with her, or if he regretted that he'd just kissed her. Jamie also averted her gaze to the coffee table by the couch, because she could feel her face flaming up again and she wanted to hide it.

She felt so awful about this whole situation, and for some reason, felt like she was to blame for it, even though she thought she had played all her cards perfectly. Filled with self-loathing and self-pity, Jamie leaned her head against Ethan and hoped that he would comfort her this one last time. But he gently pushed her away from him.

"Jamie, I think I should go."

"Wait, right now?"

He seemed to feel so awkward that he couldn't even reply.

"But . . ." She couldn't get her head straight enough to say, "How can we be kissing each other one minute and broken up the next?" Or "How could we have been *together* but not be considered boyfriend and girlfriend all this time?" Surely it wasn't supposed to happen this way. Then her mind started racing through all the plans they had in the future that would now be screwed up. What about tomorrow when they were supposed to go play laser tag at the arena in Portsmouth? Or their dinner date later in the week? Jamie felt like her whole world was collapsing, and she couldn't figure out why.

But the panic made it hard for her to breathe, much less say any of it.

Ethan rose from the couch and headed toward the door. Jamie followed close behind, praying that he'd change his mind and wrap her up in his arms for the rest of the night. But instead, he unlatched the screen door before turning to her and saying: "We *can* be friends, right, Jamie?"

Jamie was totally numb. "Sure, why not?"

"Trust me, everything is going to be just fine."

She nodded dumbly, knowing in her heart how far from the truth that was.

Ethan's frozen demeanor melted somewhat, and he reached to hug Jamie, who was only too happy to oblige. Their embrace felt normal again. No weirdness like before. Maybe now that Ethan had gotten everything out in the open, he was more relaxed. Although she wanted to stay that way forever, Jamie made herself pull away first. After all, a girl has to maintain at least a shred of dignity at a time like this.

"I'll call you," he said softly.

Jamie put her hand on his chin, as if it were the easiest, most natural thing in the world for her to do. She was relieved when he didn't pull away.

But Ethan didn't do anything else. He didn't move, or try to kiss her. He just stood there, looking like he had just broken the heart of someone he truly cared about.

They were a million miles from where they used to be.

I'm okay. I'm okay.

Jamie kept repeating this to herself every ten seconds. She figured if she chanted that long enough, she might eventually feel that way.

Jamie sat on the couch with one of her many notebooks opened on her lap. She was staring at a bad poem she'd written a couple of days ago, wondering what had motivated her to write in the first place. She tore out the page and crumpled it up in frustration, then flipped back to earlier pages, which were filled with short snippets of writing. When she'd first shown her notebooks to Ethan, it was an exhilarating experience, kind of like letting him see her naked. She was worried at first about what he'd think of her work or the pictures she'd drawn or pasted on the pages. But Ethan had loved everything that was in her notebook. It even inspired him to show her his own writing, which he kept all over the place — in boxes, binders, and manila envelopes. Reading his prose and poetry was like seeing a tender, vulnerable side of Ethan, and she'd been blown away by how talented he was. All the thoughts and dreams that he had written about were the same kinds of fantasies that she had kept secret for so long. That's when she knew there could never be anyone more right for her.

Jamie snapped herself out of her memory and brought herself back to reality. And one thing was for sure: Reality sucked. She got up to slide the glass door closed, shutting out the sounds of the summer night. She turned on the TV and Letterman was on. Was it 11:30 already? She flipped through the channels and caught flashes of NBC, Fox, and the WB. Nothing held her attention. She remembered that a few summers ago, she'd gotten up after the grown-ups had gone to bed, and sneaked downstairs to watch the *Late Late Show,* even though she was supposed to be sound asleep. She thought about how funny it was that when you were eleven or twelve, staying up past your bedtime was rebellious and daring. Things had really changed since she was a kid. She turned off the TV, shuffled into the bathroom, and splashed water on her face. Then Jamie stared at her reflection in the mirror over the sink and didn't recognize herself. Her freckles were bright dots against almost invisible skin. Her green eyes looked like they were floating in the whiteness of her face. She looked so blank. She was suddenly a nonperson. Jamie, but not Jamie.

Ethan had broken up with her.

She put her hands to her face and walked back into the living room. She sank down on the couch and touched the spot where he'd been sitting. For a year, she'd had him beside her, even when he wasn't really there. She loved his face. She loved the way he smelled. She loved a million things he'd done, or that they'd done together. Once, on the beach last summer, he'd grabbed her, pulled her onto his lap, and said, "I've got you, and I'm never letting you go."

She couldn't move. She stared out the sliding glass door, though there was nothing to see in the dark.

Finally, Jamie stood and slid her feet along the floor to her room. She didn't bother to turn on the fan. She just crawled onto the sheets and rolled onto her right side, trying to fall asleep. She heard her aunt and uncle and the kids come home. But she stayed wide awake the whole night. *I've got you,* he'd said. *And I'm never letting you go.* She kept hearing Ethan's voice echo in her ears for hours on end.

Shivering in the heat, Jamie finally cried herself to sleep as soon as the morning sun dared to show its face.

10

At Ahoy Bar and Grill downtown, Beth, Ella, Kelsi, Peter, George, and Cara (the Diet Vanilla Coke girl from the beach) were standing near the bar waiting for a table big enough to hold them all. Finally, they were given a huge booth next to a table full of college guys.

Ella squeezed in beside Beth, just across from Kelsi and Peter, while George and Cara were stuck in the curved middle portion of the seat. The red vinyl cushions sank beneath Ella as she scooted over, bumping her knee against what felt like Peter's. The fact that she couldn't play footsie with him under the table made her absolutely miserable.

"Does anybody have money for the jukebox?" Ella asked, holding out her empty palm. "I only have a twenty."

Kelsi fished in her pockets as Peter pulled out his wallet and extracted a five, laying it on Ella's tiny hand.

Ella grinned at him. "Thanks."

She squeezed out of the booth and sashayed past the table of guys next to them. On a whim, she made a pit stop there and interrupted the conversation. Of course, she hoped Peter was watching.

"Hey, would one of you mind buying me a drink? I forgot my ID." Lucky for Ella, she had her fake one tucked away in her purse, in case her charms were lost on these frat boys. But her cute little flirty smile almost always worked, and this time was no exception. At least three of them offered to get her a round.

"I'll have a Jack and Coke," she said, winking at the guy closest to her. "Don't forget."

She continued on to the jukebox, inserting the five-dollar bill. Instead of getting change, she chose fifteen of her favorite dance songs — everything from Missy Elliot and Justin Timberlake to 50 Cent and Beyoncé. On her way back, she picked up the Jack and Coke and gave the boy who'd bought it for her such a charming thank-you grin that he didn't object when she kept on walking back to her own table.

Ella, Beth, George, and Cara split fried clams and a basket of fries with vinegar. Kelsi and Peter had lasagna and calamari, which they kept picking off each other's plates. In an attempt to ignore them, Ella tried to start a game of finger football with Beth, but Beth kept turning around in her seat and asking George and Cara dumb small-talk questions like, "So you just bumped into each other again on the beach this morning? That's lucky." And "Are you in town for the whole summer, Cara?" Ella didn't know what her cousin's deal was.

Ella drummed her fingers against the table and tried to look anywhere but at Peter and Kelsi. Every few seconds, she heard kissing sounds coming from their direction, which was shocking to Ella. After all, Kelsi was the poster girl for the anti-PDA movement. Hearing them kiss made Ella want to run screaming out of the bar. Her only consolation was the thought that kissing was probably *all* Kelsi and Peter ever did.

Some college kids had started congregating in an empty area of the room near the bar. They began to dance to the selection of tunes Ella had picked out. She couldn't help but be proud of her stint as DJ. The people out on the floor were loving the music and seemed to be having so much fun that Ella wolfed down the last of her share of clams so that she could join in. She stood up and peered down at Cara and George.

"You guys wanna dance?"

"I'm kind of nursing this surfboard injury." George shook his head and pointed to his left ankle. "Maybe later?"

Cara also declined the invitation very politely. "I don't really ever dance on a full stomach."

Ella rolled her eyes at both of them and let out an exasperated sigh. She slid out of the booth and stood at the end of the bench across from Beth. She started dancing and mouthing the words to a J.Lo song, then waggled a come-hither finger. Damn it, she was going to accomplish Mission Forget Peter. And she was going to have fun doing it.

She winked and made a goofy kissy face at Beth, sensing that the guys at the next table were watching her and hoping she'd give them a good show.

"Come on, sweet stuff," she said to Beth, tossing her shiny mane of blonde hair back and forth as if she were in a shampoo commercial.

She stretched out her hand, and Beth finally accepted. They

moved toward the crowd and stood on the edge for a few seconds, then slowly started to move in when the moment felt right. Ella's favorite thing in the universe (next to Dentyne Ice and boys) was dancing, so when the bass line really began to pulsate, she immediately picked up her pace. Dancing just made her body feel free.

In fact, Ella was so caught up in the fluid motion of the crowd that she hardly noticed when George and Cara drifted up to the edge of the makeshift dance floor. Her seductive moves were creating a lot of commotion around her. Practically every guy was coming up to Ella one by one, as if they'd all taken a number at the deli, dancing so close that they were almost touching her. Ella exchanged glances with Beth, and asked with her expression what she thought of each guy. Either Beth shook her head, or smirked and rolled her eyes, or missed it altogether because she was so busy watching George and Cara.

A hand tapped Ella on the shoulder. When she turned around, she was looking at a tall, blond guy, very hunky, with bright blue eyes that were focused only on her.

"Can I buy you another one of those?" he said, pointing at her glass, which only had a small splash of Jack and Coke lingering at the bottom.

He was perfect — just a little bit yuppie in his khaki pants and polo shirt, just a little bit rebel with his gelled hair and devilish grin. He was just what Ella had ordered.

"Definitely," she said, with a sassy twist of her lips.

Ella could feel the knot in her stomach untying and her body filling with relief. She was in control of herself again. She only glanced at Kelsi and Peter once as she followed Perfect Guy to the bar. Kelsi had her hands on Peter's knees, and Peter's fingers twirled her short, flat hair.

Ella didn't care anymore. She really didn't.

There was a new boy in town.

They burst out of Ahoy at 11:30, drenched in so much party sweat, it looked as if they'd been hosed down by the local fire department. They'd missed the fireworks, but nobody seemed to care.

Ella linked her arm through Beth's for the hot, three-block walk back to the car. Perfect Guy, whose real name was Brad, had asked for her number, and she'd happily given it to him. She felt triumphant and giddy as the group made their way down the cobblestone street.

When they finally arrived at the car, everyone piled in like a bunch of circus clowns. George was driving, so Cara sat shotgun. Ella could have found another place to sit, but she plunked down on top of Peter's lap, even though Kelsi was sitting right next to him. Sure, she was over him. Definitely over him. But still, there was nothing more satisfying to Ella than watching her older sister squirm a bit.

It was quiet on the way back. Everyone was exhausted from dancing, so each of them seemed to fall into their own little worlds. In the dark, Ella could feel the warmth of Peter's legs under hers. For a brief moment, she tried to imagine what it would be like if she was really his girlfriend, and she was sitting on his lap back at his place.

Ella's little fantasy was cut short when the plastic part of one of the seatbelts kept brushing against her. She shifted and for a second it was gone, and then back again. How annoying. She looked down at her short pink cotton skirt, and realized that the plastic part of the seatbelt was actually Peter's thumb pressed lightly against the side of her right thigh.

Uh, what the hell is going on? screamed a voice inside Ella's head.

Clearly, he didn't know what he was doing. He had had some drinks at the bar and his judgment had obviously been severely affected. *That was the only rational explanation for this, right?* Ella thought frantically. Or perhaps this is what Peter had been wanting to do all along?

Ella felt her ears start to burn. She wondered if her skin was as hot as it suddenly felt, and if he could feel her body heat smoldering through his jeans. She was embarrassed that he might. How could he not? She tried to remember the Ella of a few minutes ago, who'd taken charge of her life, and forget that his hand was anywhere near her thigh.

She stole a glance to her left. Kelsi had nodded off to sleep, her right hand entwined with Peter's left, which leaned lazily against the armrest. Kelsi looked so trusting, it made Ella feel even worse that she didn't want Peter to take his hand away.

And he didn't. Suddenly, Peter's fingers started to move. They traced over her skin in a delicate pattern. The sensation brought Ella's skin to almost unbearable heat. She could feel the roughness of his knuckles tickle every single nerve ending. Back and forth, back and forth.

It was a deliberate and stealthy rhythm, very much like the way he walked.

11

Jamie lay on her stomach, on the knotted pink quilt that covered her bed, listening to Jeff Buckley. Her back was covered with yellow slices where the sun peeked at her body through the blinds. "Lover, You Should Have Come Over" was on repeat on her stereo. It had played six times so far.

She was vaguely aware that the summer was passing her by. It was already mid-July. Her mother had come and gone once, floating in and out of Pebble Beach like a dust cloud and leaving Jamie hoards of Tupperware containers filled with various salads.

Jamie was also vaguely aware that the phone was ringing. Slowly, she reached down to the cordless receiver, which she'd stolen from the living room and held hostage in her bedroom for ten days. Lifting her head for a second, she could feel the places where the knots had dug into the skin of her face.

"Hello?"

"J, it's me." Ethan's voice came over the line without a hint of cellular static. He sounded wonderful. Jamie sat up and cleared her throat as her skin went clammy.

"Hi," Jamie whispered.

"Hey, I know it's been a while since we've talked. But I'm having a party tomorrow, and I wanted to know if you wanted to come. You could bring your cousins."

Jamie nodded, and then remembered Ethan couldn't see her. They were on a phone, not speaking to each other via satellite. "Ummm," she said.

"I thought it'd be cool to hang out. I feel like I haven't seen you in a year, J."

"Um." Jamie searched the far reaches of her brain for a coherent thought. She wanted to see him so badly, she was actually getting a physical pain in her chest.

"Are you sure you want me to come?" she managed to sputter.

"Of course I do," he said cheerfully. "It'll be fun."

Jamie tugged at a knot on the quilt until she pulled it out, leaving a ragged little hole in the fabric. Her fingers were trembling. *Fun. Fun is good.*

She managed to control her voice enough to get her question out. "Ethan, do you mean you want me to come as . . . just a friend?"

"Well, aren't we friends?" Ethan asked in return.

Jamie was completely stumped. Were they?

"I guess," she replied wistfully.

"Okay, then. Will you come to my party?"

Say no, say no. Jamie knew she should refuse. The only thing that might be worse than not seeing Ethan, would be pretending that she was fine with being his friend. But even though that reasonable part of Jamie was begging her not to cave, the need to see Ethan again was much bigger than her fear of falling apart when she did. "Yeah. Yeah, I'll come."

"Great. See you then."

Jamie swallowed the rest of the questions she wanted to ask. "See you. Bye."

After she hung up, she slammed her cheek back onto the mattress. He'd called. She couldn't believe it. Part of her really wanted to call him and tell him she'd changed her mind, but another part of her was excited that she was on *his* mind. He hadn't forgotten about her.

Grabbing a pen and a piece of scrap paper from beside the phone, Jamie started sketching. She wanted to get all her feelings out on paper — she found this to be very therapeutic. She drew a cartoon Jamie with a fire poker stoking some flames burning beneath her rib cage. She drew a pair of hands squeezing the inside of her chest. She drew a rake scraping down the sidewalk.

Then she crumpled the paper and threw it at the picture of Ethan she'd jammed into the corner of her dresser mirror. She'd have to burn that soon. Once she got out of bed — if that ever, ever happened again.

There was a knock at the door. "Jamie?" It was Ella.

Jamie groaned and buried her face in the pillow.

"Jamie, let me in. I think you're about to fall into the void."

"Go away, all right, Ella?" Jamie said, feeling the tears well up now that somebody was around to hear her cry. She'd expected Ella to show up at some point. She could be selfish sometimes, but Ella was a mother hen at heart.

"You can't stay in there forever," Ella insisted.

"Why not?" Jamie rolled over and faced the window.

She could still hear Ella out there, sighing dramatically. "I'll be back," she said firmly, and her footsteps sounded down the hall.

There was no telling how long she'd been sleeping when Jamie woke to a scratching at the door. At first, dazed, she thought it was a cat. Then the doorknob turned, and Ella appeared in a pink tank top and gray Juicy sweatshorts, holding a bulging plastic bag in one hand and a bobby pin that she'd used to pick the lock in the other.

"We can do this the healthy way or the trashy way," she said, walking up to the bed, dropping the bag beside Jamie, and tucking the bobby pin into her hair. "But we're definitely doing it."

Jamie couldn't help feeling a little curious. She sat up and rubbed her eyes. A major head rush followed. She felt like she'd been run over by a bulldozer.

Ella was carefully extracting the items from her bag: a video (*Legally Blonde,* one of Ella's favorites), a tube of Queen Helene's Mint Julep facial mask, a cucumber, a tiny glass tub of Pink Pepper nail polish, a pack of minicigars, and what no feel-better care package would ever be complete without — a small bottle of tangerine-flavored Stoli vodka.

Jamie rubbed her face again. "I'm looking for the common thread here."

Ella started separating the things into two piles. "I was thinking we could do a spa night — mask and makeovers and a movie . . . ," she said while spreading everything out onto the bed. "Or we can drink and smoke cigars and play poker." She pulled out a pack of cards from her back pocket. Jamie recognized them from the trunk of games in the living room. Ella held up the cards and the video, moving them up and down like they were on scales, her eyebrows high and questioning.

Jamie was surprised to feel her soul emerge from the darkness for a second. "Can't we do both?"

Ella threw back her head and laughed. "Whatever you say."

"Hey, where is everybody?"

Ella took a quick look at the clock. It was 4:35. "Down at the beach, where else? Then dinner at our house. So let's get cracking. We don't have all day!"

The afternoon sun was shining dimly through the blinds. Jamie swung her legs over the side of the bed, then stood up and pulled the cord for the fan. Then she locked the door again.

"I'll take one of those cigars," Jamie said, setting herself up against the headboard.

Ella smiled at her as she opened the window to let the smoke out. Jamie found the energy to smile back.

They hunkered down on the bed and took swigs straight from the bottle. Ella dealt the cards, but stopped halfway through to veto the Jeff Buckley CD.

"What *is* this shit?" she said, switching it off and turning the knob to radio. She surfed the channels until she found a Jay-Z song, then cranked up the volume to an eardrum-thumping level.

"What you gotta do is forget that loser," Ella shouted above the music, crawling back onto the bed and dealing the rest of the cards. She fanned hers out in front of her eyes. Jamie tapped her cigar on a bowl on the nightstand.

"Forget him," Jamie repeated hollowly.

"Yeah, there are plenty of guys out there that are way, way better than him. Did you ever notice how nasty his feet are? I did."

The thought of being with anyone else was ludicrous to Jamie. But Ella's spirit was contagious. She half laughed.

"He invited me to a party tomorrow. For some reason, he thinks we can be friends. I don't know if maybe he still likes me, or something . . ." Jamie trailed off.

"Jamie," Ella said, leveling a gaze over her cards. "It's the classic guy maneuver. He wants to have you even when he doesn't have you. He wants to be broken up, but he still wants you to be crazy over him."

Jamie took a sip of Stoli. "Or maybe he still likes me."

"Maybe," Ella said sympathetically, as Jamie took a double swig. "So you're going, huh?"

"I said I would. But I don't know, maybe I shouldn't have."

"Well, look, it's hard to stay away. I get it. But if you're gonna be around him, you've at least got to show him you don't need him. You've got to show him you're interested in other things. Guys are stupid like that. They love it when girls act like they don't want them." Ella nodded her head wisely.

Jamie tried to picture herself not wanting Ethan.

"Ella, I just feel like I can't breathe," she said as tears stung her eyes. She felt like such a baby, crying again.

Ella scooted over to comfort her, and rubbed Jamie's back gently. "It sucks. I know, I know," she said.

Jamie was kind of embarrassed that she was allowing Ella to see her like this, but the vodka had created a soothing warmth in her chest, and the back rub felt good. But what she appreciated most was that Ella was doing all she could to make Jamie feel as if she was being understood. After all, Ella was a dumper, not a dumpee. She'd never had her heart broken in her life. Yet here she was, giving Jamie a sympathetic shoulder to cry on.

A few tears slipped out onto Jamie's hands and dripped onto her shirt, leaving behind a little trail of misery. Her curly hair stuck to her face. When she lifted her head, Ella turned her toward the mirror near her bed.

"Nice mustache," she said.

They both smiled weakly at Jamie's reflection, then Jamie wiped the hair away and bit her lip.

"Ella, you don't understand. It's like I can't see anything but him." She realized how melodramatic she sounded. "I mean, have you ever felt that way about anyone?" Jamie looked at her hopefully, like a drowning person looking desperately for a life raft. Maybe there was some formula for surviving this, and only Ella had the answer.

Ella looked thoughtful and a little sad. "Nope. I mean I've been, like, infatuated. But I don't think I've ever felt the real thing — you know, love."

"I thought I had that with Ethan. . . ."

"I know. I'm sorry. Listen, I'll give you a makeover for the party. You'll look fabulous, and he'll eat his heart out."

Jamie swallowed, feeling shy all over again.

"But now you need another cigar," Ella said winningly, holding out the box.

"Oh, God, no," Jamie waved her away. She was already worried the room reeked. She picked up the vodka instead.

"Bottoms up," Ella said with a lilt to her voice. "You only live once."

*   *   *

They got good and drunk. At least Jamie did. Before this, she had only experienced a good buzz, and when she did, it was usually after 9:00 P.M. But this was a special occasion.

Ella and Jamie played several hands of cards and then just talked, laughing over old stories. It was the best Jamie had felt in days. By the time it got dark, she and Ella had curled up in the bed and popped in the movie, and soon she began to sober up.

A couple of hours later, her aunt and uncle got home with the kids. She could hear them walking in the hall, tucking the kids in, and then making their way into the common room, where they turned on the TV. Ella was lying beside her, fast asleep, snoring in the blue glow of the TV as the tape went into automatic rewind mode. Watching her, Jamie noticed a thin thread of drool dangling from her cousin's perfect mouth, and she snickered a bit. Still, the quiet laugh gave way to silence. In a full house, with her cousin in her bed, Jamie knew she was surrounded by people who cared about her. But she felt completely alone.

12

Ella pulled into the parking lot behind the Okay Café downtown and yanked on the parking brake. She checked her face in the visor mirror to make sure everything looked picture-perfect and smiled at herself. For the first time in two weeks, she didn't have puffy bags tugging at the delicate skin under her eyes. She'd finally slept, a little, thanks to Mr. Vodka. It seemed a little dysfunctional, but what the hell.

When she got out of the car, Ella stretched her arms above her head. She felt so refreshed and happy that the kinks in her stomach had finally loosened up.

It had been a few weeks since Peter had touched her in the car. Since then, Ella's mind had gone wild, creating scenarios that kept her awake night after night. Every day she hadn't seen him — every time Kelsi went off to meet him somewhere — had made it worse. But because of her girls' night in with Jamie, she suddenly felt back to normal. Up until now, Ella had been hoping Peter would show up on her doorstep, or that they'd run into each other somewhere. But because he hadn't, it made everything easier. Ella was going to move on and be done with this whole insane crush of hers.

The café was virtually empty, so it was easy to spot Kelsi at a table by the window. She was reading a folded newspaper. Her sunglasses were tucked on top of her head and her legs were crossed loosely at the ankle. She was wearing a gauzy white hippie-style tank top and khaki shorts. Ella watched her for a second, wondering what Peter saw in her exactly. And then Kelsi met her eyes.

"Hey." She waved to catch Ella's attention.

Ella made her way to the table, then plopped down and dropped her straw tote beside her chair.

Kelsi waved the newspaper at her.

"Did you know that even though the sun is about four hundred times bigger than the moon," she said, "the distance between them makes them appear almost exactly the same size to us on Earth?"

Ella shrugged and looked behind her for the waiter.

"That's why we can have total eclipses," Kelsi said, looking back down at the article. "It's a huge coincidence, like two puzzle pieces. . . ."

"Cool."

"Some people think it's proof of a divine plan at work."

"I guess," Ella agreed. Actually, the word *divine* made Ella think of Peter's back muscles.

The waiter, a Steve Buscemi clone, walked up and hovered over them.

"One napoleon, two forks," Kelsi said, throwing a glance at

Ella. "And two iced café au laits." It was the only thing they ever got here. They came to the Okay Café for napoleons at least three times a summer. It was sort of a sisterly tradition.

"We should go by the Look Out Diner after this to hang out with Peter." Kelsi folded her newspaper tighter and stuffed it into her worn, purple JanSport knapsack.

A flame leaped in Ella's stomach. Just the mere mention of his name was enough to do that to her.

Kelsi put her chin on her hand and looked out the window. "Don't you think he's incredible?"

Ella fumbled over her words. "I . . . uh . . . I dunno." A sudden image of Peter with his hand on her thigh flashed into her mind. Thankfully the waiter arrived with their pastry and set it down between them, then placed the two tall glasses of coffee in front of them. It snapped Ella out of her trance. "If you like butt chins," she finally managed to say as she dug into the napoleon with her fork.

Kelsi laughed. "I guess he does have a butt chin." She looked thoughtful, her brown eyes focused on something beyond Ella's shoulder. "But I think it's sexy."

"Hmm." Ella dug harder into the pastry, sneaking her fork over onto Kelsi's half.

"Here," Kelsi pushed the plate toward her. "You know, I'm not even hungry."

When Ella had wolfed down the whole pastry and finished her glass of coffee, Kelsi asked for the check. She studied it for a second, then laid down a five-dollar bill and three singles, plus a handful of change. "My treat," she said, pushing back her chair and standing up.

They walked out of the café and turned left, Kelsi leading the way toward the diner. That morning, when Ella had gotten dressed, she'd had the possibility in mind that she might see Peter, like she'd had every day since the Fourth of July. She'd put on her tight turquoise tank top with the double spaghetti straps and black capris, thinking of him. She'd worn her lacy black thong underneath just because.

But seeing him with Kelsi wasn't what she'd fantasized about. She nervously reached for her pack of Dentyne Ice, wishing she could have a cigarette instead.

When they got to the door of the diner, Kelsi smoothed back her hair with both hands. Ella fought the urge to do the same. A pretty blonde stood at the hostess podium, marking something with a pen. She looked up at them with a hint of hostility. Ella glared right back. Girls like that were often bitchy to her off the bat. It was like an Old West showdown. *This town isn't big enough for the both of us.*

"Is Peter around?" Kelsi asked the hostess as she shoved her hands in the front pockets of her shorts.

The girl shook her head. "Not until four."

Kelsi looked disappointed as they walked back out onto the sidewalk. They made their way up Main Street, aimless now. Ella had the sudden urge to reach out and hug her sister and apologize for everything mean she'd ever done to her. Like the time she'd put shoe polish in her shampoo. And the time she'd made all her friends join the "I Hate Kelsi Club" out of jealousy that they might like her better than Ella. Ella told herself she could ignore what had happened with Peter. She could resist temptations. All she needed was a little more will power.

"I love that," Kelsi said, pausing in front of a lingerie shop with one finger at the corner of her mouth. Her lips were curved up in a smile. Kelsi's smiles never used to *curve.* "Don't you?"

The lingerie on display in the store's front window was a cropped see-through lace top and sexy, frilled underwear in a deep emerald green. It reminded Ella of something a naughty French cancan dancer might wear, but in a good way. Classy, vintagey, but sexy. "Um, you mean, for you?"

"Yeah."

"You mean, to buy?"

"No, I mean to just stand out here and gawk at," Kelsi said with a laugh. "Let's go in," she said decidedly.

Ella trailed after her, feeling suddenly queasy. Their mom always took Kelsi shopping at the Maidenform place at the mall, where the bras offered support. Here, they clearly offered something a little bit more. It was the kind of place Ella had never envisioned her sister shopping at. It was a shop for *women who have sex.*

Kelsi was already studying the white tag that hung from the set on the mannequin. "I think I'm gonna get it," she said. "What do you think?"

"What do I think?" Ella ran through the mental catalog of possible things she could say. Her head was spinning. There was no reason for Kelsi to buy lingerie. She thought of Peter, burying his head in Kelsi's neck at the bar. She imagined Peter looking at Kelsi naked.

"El?"

"Um, don't you think it's a little . . . *racy?* " She could feel one of her mom's signature words rolling out of her mouth.

Kelsi looked very amused. "Thank you, Mary Poppins. Of course. It's sexy."

Ella wondered if her face was turning red. "I guess. If you're into . . . that."

Kelsi ignored Ella's unenthusiastic response and kept scanning the rack for a set that was her size. Ella ran her hands through the racks, too, touching this lacy thong, that satin bra, absentmindedly. She wondered what was Peter's favorite color.

Her hand landed on a cinnamon-red strapless demi-bra. The upper half of it was meshy and see-through. It had twice the sex appeal of the green set, and half the class.

She didn't hesitate, or figure out how she'd ever wear it for the person she was thinking of. She sifted through the matching thongs, plucking out a medium. She'd save it for a rainy day.

Ella slid the items onto the counter just as Kelsi had finished paying, and took out her wallet. Kelsi eyed Ella's purchase, surprised, as the lady rang it up. Ella braced herself for a lecture — something big sisterly about her not being old enough for sexy lingerie. But Kelsi didn't say anything at all.

Obviously, she had more important things on her mind.

13

"Have you seen my deodorant?"

George was standing in Beth's bedroom doorway, his face flushed from the hot shower he'd just taken. He had a towel wrapped around his waist.

Beth was in front of the mirror, trying to fasten a bracelet she had never gotten around to wearing because she always had trouble putting the damn thing on. They were getting ready for the party at Ethan's house.

"You put it under your pillow, remember?" she said.

George nodded. "Oh, yeah." He'd put it there so he'd remember to use it in the mornings. He looked at her wrist. "You want some help with that?"

Beth eyed herself in the mirror. "No, I got it."

"Here," George stepped up behind her and turned her around, holding tight to his towel with one hand, then tucking it in tighter so that both hands were free. He took hold of her wrist.

"I do this for my mom all the time," he said, concentrating very hard on the tiny little clasp.

George had long fingers and bulky knuckles, so Beth didn't know how long this was going to take. She watched his hand as it worked open the clasp and expertly hooked it through the eye of the chain. She stared at the drops of water on his chest, and listened to his deep and steady breath.

"Wow, Cara. You were right," she muttered.

"What's that?" George asked.

Beth could feel her cheeks burning. Had she actually said that *out loud*?

"I said, thanks, George," she said quickly, then turned her back to him.

"No problem. Don't mention it."

"Is Miss Violin Virtuoso coming tonight?" Beth asked, teasingly, though she still felt flushed.

"Yes, Miss Pain-in-My-Ass. She should be here any minute."

"Oh." Beth was trying to feel happy for George, but once again there were these surprising emotions lurking around inside her that she just wasn't prepared to deal with. At least not yet.

"Beth?"

"Yeah?" She glanced over at him.

George shifted from foot to foot nervously. "Maybe, you know, you could talk to her? I don't know if we're just friends or what."

Beth nervously tugged at her top as she eyed him in the mirror.

"Really?"

"I mean, maybe you could try to find out if she likes me."

Beth shrugged. Being a girl herself, it was pretty obvious that

Cara liked George. She'd given him her number. She'd come to Ahoy on Fourth of July. She kept coming to their spot on the beach to sunbathe and drink Diet Vanilla Cokes, and she'd even come by the cottage a couple of times.

"Sure, I'll see what I can pry out of her," Beth said in her most sisterly sounding voice. She didn't want him to see right through her.

"Cool," George said, and then placed a goofy wet kiss on Beth's cheek. He dashed out the door to his own room, next door, where she heard him call out. "You're the best, babe!"

Beth studied herself in the mirror. Her hair was pulled back in a loose braid. She was wearing a dark blue halter top meant to downplay the size of her boobs, and an aqua-green homemade skirt she'd borrowed from Jamie. On Jamie, it looked loose and sort of gamine. On Beth, it was tight and short, but that wasn't necessarily a bad thing. She had nice long, muscular legs — even if they were dotted with tiny bruises from surfing. Why hadn't George commented on how good she looked?

Because he's an idiot, that's why, she thought to herself. Besides, maybe George was right about summer boys. Maybe this was her time to act, and it was flying by while she was busy having these conflicting thoughts — about her best friend, of all people! She just had to take the first step and actually make an effort. And the sooner the better.

Then, out of nowhere, Beth thought of George again. She realized he was probably naked in the room next door, and she pictured him drying himself off with the towel. She shook her head, hard. Was she going insane?

"George, I'll meet you outside," she called to him as she

headed for the door. She absolutely had to put some distance between herself and George's nudity. Just above the light switch in Beth's room, there was a shelf holding a fisherman figurine carved out of cork. Last summer, George had dubbed him Chauncy. Beth turned out the light, patted his captain's hat for luck, and then headed down the hall, trying to pretend the last few seconds hadn't happened.

Outside, the sky was slightly purple, but the moon was giving off just enough light for Beth to see the group already gathered on the porch next door. The air was still pretty hot and muggy.

Jamie was standing on the porch in what looked like one of Ella's outfits — a skirt that stopped halfway down her thighs and a strappy black tank top. Her hair was pulled back at the top, but some of it hung loose and curly over her shoulders, and as Beth got closer, she could see she was wearing makeup. She looked vampy, except that she was tugging at her curls self-consciously. She was talking to someone, and it took Beth a second to see that it was Cara.

"Hey, guys," Beth said as she approached them slowly.

"Beth, you look great," Jamie said in a very strained-sounding voice.

"Thanks." Beth was already looking at Cara, sizing her up. She was wearing khaki clam diggers and a red strapless top. Her penny-colored hair was pulled back in a sleek ponytail. Beth felt whatever amount of confidence she'd had a few moments ago plummet like an out-of-control elevator.

Beth tried to shake off the negative vibes. She was used to being eclipsed by the girls around her, who were smaller and girlier and softer. It wasn't a big deal. "Where are Ella and Kelsi?" she asked.

"Not coming," Jamie answered. "Kelsi has a date with Peter, and Ella is seeing that guy she met at Ahoy."

When George came out a few minutes later, his hair combed and his skin looking scrubbed, his eyes lingered on Cara for a moment longer than on anyone else. Then he headed for the car. He was driving.

"Well," Jamie said, already walking down the steps to the car. "Let's get going. It's now or never." She tossed her hair in a distinctly un-Jamie-like manner.

Beth got the sense that this was one party Jamie definitely didn't want to miss.

There were about seventy people streaming out of Ethan's living room onto his back deck and out onto the lawn. There was a group of people dancing in the living room, holding beers in their hands and bobbing to classic rock music. Some guy wearing a sailor's hat was tending bar across the room.

Beth tugged down the hem of her skirt and scanned the crowd for boys with potential. "Solid talent," is what George would have called it. She was going to meet someone tonight — she could just feel it.

"I'll be back," Jamie said almost immediately after she entered the room, her eyes wide and hopeful as they searched for any sign of Ethan. She headed into the mass of people, her hips swaying as she walked.

"Jamie's looking hot tonight," George said, watching her as

she skipped off into the crowd. "Not that I was really noticing," he covered, turning to Cara and blushing.

It was extremely easy to tell when George blushed because he was so pale. Beth looked at him with Cara and wondered why he had never blushed like that with her.

After standing around for a couple of minutes surveying the damage already done to Ethan's place, the three of them gravitated to one of the brown, velvety couches by the open archway of the living room. George and Cara immediately turned toward each other, leaving Beth sitting alone beside George.

"So how did you become interested in the violin, anyway?" George asked Cara in his most mature voice. Beth leaned over George's shoulder so she could feel like a part of things.

"Oh, I was raised on the violin," Cara said as stroked her ponytail with one hand. "My parents started me on the Suzuki method when I was four."

"Four, wow."

"The joke in my family," Cara smiled mirthfully, "is that my first word wasn't Mama, it was Yo Yo Mama."

"Ha!" George grabbed both his knees with the force of his laugh. "That's a good one. Yo Yo Mama. Man, that's funny."

Oh God. With all her strength, Beth fought the urge to roll her eyes. Cara was the kind of girl George and Beth might have made fun of a few weeks ago. Serious, boring, and ridiculously cheesy. Who knew George would be so totally into her? It made Beth disappointed in him that he could fall for someone so blah. But her disapproval made her feel guilty. And then she got annoyed with George for making her feel disappointed *and* guilty. Then she considered seeking psychiatric help for her split personality disorder, which was worsening every minute she spent sitting there listening to them gab on and on about nothing.

Cara said she was on a diet and George pinched her arm and told her she shouldn't be, which made Cara pinch him back and say, "You're so sweet." Beth thought about going outside and throwing herself under the next car that drove by. She nodded her head to the music, trying to look occupied, but that could only go on for so long. Finally, she looked at the bar and realized she'd found an escape.

"Who wants drinks?" she asked, jumping out of her seat excitedly. George and Cara didn't seem to hear. "I know I do," she said out loud to herself, because no one seemed to notice that she existed.

Beth nearly tripped over a couple making out on a chair at the edge of the dance floor. The guy had his hand on the girl's thigh and they were practically sucking each other's faces off. Beth cringed. People could be so gross.

At the bar, Sailor Hat guy was still mixing cocktails for everyone. He kept bobbing around the bar, half-filling drinks and handing them out, having a grand time, but looking overwhelmed.

When his eyes met Beth's, she leaned in to order the drinks. Then she realized this was an opportunity to let loose and have a little fun.

"You want some help?" she asked, instead of ordering.

"From a pretty girl like you? Hell, yeah!" he said with a grin. Beth thanked him with an unusually girly giggle. "Do you know anything about mixing drinks?" he asked.

Beth shrugged. "It's like math, isn't it? Ten percent this, fifty percent that."

"Right, close enough," Sailor Hat guy said and scooted over, indicating that the space beside him was hers.

"What do you want?" she asked the first person she made eye contact with, a redhaired girl.

"What can you make?"

Beth looked at what she had to work with: half-empty bottles of vodka, rum, cranberry and orange juices, Coke. Plus, the ever-popular beer of choice, Bud Lite.

"Basically, the staples."

From then on, whoever wanted a mixed drink got a screwdriver, a rum and Coke, or a vodka cranberry, regardless of what they asked for. Beth made herself a drink and sipped at it between making everyone else's.

"You're good," Sailor Hat guy said with a hint of awe in his voice. Beth reveled in the pleasant sensation of being watched with admiration.

At least now she had a *purpose*. She was the bartender and everybody loved her. One partygoer called her Captain Jack and her sidekick Sailor Joe. Jamie appeared, demanded two drinks, and gave Beth a sloppy kiss on the cheek. It was worlds better than sitting with George and Yo Yo Mama. Before Beth knew it, an hour had gone by and she was wrapped in the embrace of a nice buzz, only a tiny bit worried that the liquor was almost gone and that she might have to stop being Captain Jack all too soon.

She got a clear view of the brown velvet couch at one point, when she ducked for a cooler of ice. Through the spaces between people's bodies she could see George and Cara sitting there, oblivious to the fact that she'd never come back. If they sat any closer, they could have combined into one giant cell through osmosis.

She stood back up and noticed two of her bottles were empty. Damn. She glanced around quickly, trying to improvise. All she saw were half-empty cups that people had left lying around.

She grabbed several of the cups in the immediate vicinity and carried them back to the bar. It was easy to tell which drink was which from her limited repertoire. She started pouring the glasses into each other. It brought a huge smile to her lips. *I'm saving the party,* she thought to herself. Sailor Hat guy, who'd introduced himself as Alex, followed her lead, once again clearly impressed with her ingenuity. Beth felt like a hero.

When George and Cara finally drifted up to the bar, George had his hand on Cara's back, massaging it lightly. Beth tried not to look. She swiped at the hair in her eyes and noticed for the first time that she was sweating. Her outfit clung to her and there were two huge wet spots where she'd spilled drinks on her chest. Very, very classy. Cara, on the other hand, looked cool as a cucumber.

"What do you want?" George asked Cara, as if they were at a real bar. He wasn't drinking, since he was driving them home.

"You should probably have the beer," Beth offered, more generous than she wanted to be.

"Why?"

She gave a conspiratorial wink to her cobartender. It wouldn't hurt for George to see her flirting. "Because the only liquor we're serving is recycled." George eyed the empty cups littering the bar, seeming to get what she meant almost immediately. He had to explain it to Cara.

"Oh." She wrinkled her nose, looking slightly disgusted.

"Beth," George said quietly, "that's kinda gross."

The grin disappeared from Beth's face.

"It's funny," she said, hearing the flatness in her own voice. At least she didn't sound as hurt as she felt.

"I guess," Cara said in a condescending tone that totally enraged Beth. But instead of reaching over and spilling one of the cups over Cara's head, Beth maintained her composure and just closed her jaw tight.

She looked at Alex for validation. But he had backed away a few feet and was talking to a girl in a tight sundress. "I'm saving the party," she finally said, forlornly.

Cara took her beer and walked away with George.

Captain Jack stood alone, suddenly wishing that she had just stayed home.

"So Jamie wouldn't come with you?" George asked solemnly, knitting his eyebrows in concern. They were driving home from the party, and turning onto Route 41, which was a straight, three-minute shot to their section of Pebble Beach.

"She was talking to some guy. She swore she was spending the night," Beth said from the backseat. Cara was up front, of course.

"Beth, you should have made her come."

"I tried. But, you know, she knows all those people. Ethan's friends. I'm sure she's fine. It's only a few minutes drive away anyway. She could practically walk home."

"I guess so," George said, looking unconvinced. "Still, I'd feel better if she were coming home with us."

"She's fine," Beth reiterated sternly before gnawing on her lower lip. It wasn't as if George had taken the time to even find Jamie, much less try to make her come home. He'd been too busy flirting with Cara.

Beth looked out at the road and the darkness zooming by. They'd left the party long before it looked like it would wind down because her mom had asked them to be home by 1:00. But even if they didn't have a curfew, Beth would have been more than happy to leave.

The only thing she wanted to do was to get in her room, close the door, and be by herself. When they pulled into the driveway, the three of them quietly spilled out of the car. The night had finally cooled down, and the sound of the waves was actually quite soothing after the noise of the party.

Beth started toward the cottage door as Cara began walking to her own cottage, farther up the road. George hesitated between them.

"You guys wanna hang out a while longer?" he asked, directing the question mostly toward Cara. Beth's abdomen started to throb. She wanted George to come inside and be with her and make fun of the party like they always did. They could dig her dad's macaroni salad out of the fridge and chat for a while.

"Sure," Cara said, pushing the toe of one foot into the ground contentedly.

"I'm exhausted," Beth said, stretching out her arms to underline the point. "I'm going in."

Please come in, George. Please come in.

She was losing him. She'd felt it all night long. She was losing her best friend to a Diet-Vanilla-Coke–drinking, boring-ass violinist.

"Cool," he said. "Good night, Bethy." George took Cara by the arm and escorted her to the picnic table at the far side of the lawn.

Beth thought about changing her mind and parking herself right between the two of them until they both got annoyed and went home. But that wouldn't be fair to George.

So she swallowed the lump in her throat and walked inside alone.

14

The first thing Jamie did when she separated from Beth and the others at the party was stop by the bar. At the very least, she wanted to have a drink in her hand. She wanted to look casual. The more at ease she appeared, the better chance she had of winning Ethan back. That had been Ella's logic. It didn't seem quite sensible to Jamie, but then, where had her own logic gotten her so far?

"What'll you have?" The Sailor Hat guy who was mixing the drinks gave her an openly appreciative smile that was aimed mostly at her legs. Jamie shifted from foot to foot.

"Something with vodka, please." Nervous under the guy's gaze, she scanned the room, her eyes landing on a full-length mirror a few feet away, on a wall beside the kitchen. She could see her reflection staring back at her, but she barely recognized herself. Her green eyes were lined with kohl, which made them look more catlike than ever. The flimsy black top clung to her torso, a bare sliver of flesh showing below her collarbone and also on either side of her waist, where the hem of the shirt curved up revealingly.

Her legs were long and coltish under the skirt, which barely covered her upper thighs. No wonder the bartender was staring.

"Here you go. One screwdriver," he said, thrusting the cup in front of her.

"Thanks." It was filled to the brim, with a few melting ice cubes floating on top. Jamie stepped away from the bar, took two long sips and surveyed the room a second time. She felt as if her heart was lodged in her throat. She was sure Ethan was somewhere close by. She bobbed her head to the music just in case he was watching her from some hiding place in another room.

Just keep acting cool, she thought to herself.

Pushing her shoulders back and picking up her confidence, she sauntered from the kitchen to the dining room to the hallway. She didn't want to find Ethan so much as bump into him. As she walked, she tried to look sexy and careless, like Ella always did. She sipped her screwdriver at regular intervals. She'd already drunk two-thirds of it when she found him, standing among a circle of people in the den downstairs, talking animatedly and waving his arms. Jamie stood in the doorway, just on the verge of entering the room. She'd spent so much time working on looking good tonight that she hadn't even anticipated how amazing *Ethan* would look. She was overwhelmed by how much she still cared about him.

"Jamie." Ethan had pulled himself back slightly from the group and was waving her over. Jamie swallowed, and then willed her feet forward.

Once she got to the circle, he wrapped her up in a hug. He smelled like he'd just taken a swim in the ocean. "I'm glad you made it. Are you here with your cousins?"

Jamie nodded. "Yeah, they're all upstairs." It would be better not to mention that she'd left them all in the dust as soon as she'd walked in the door.

Ethan took a couple of minutes to study her. "Damn. You're looking good tonight," he said with that toothy grin that always gave her goose bumps. "I want you to meet some people."

Taking her hand in his, Ethan introduced her around the circle, to a skinny brunette with ultra-short bangs, to a guy with bright blue eyes and high cheekbones, and to a girl in a striped tube top. Jamie smoothed back her curly hair and smiled at everyone. Ethan immediately launched back into the gripping speech he'd been giving to the whole group. He was talking about going scuba diving next year in Australia, where he'd spent some time before.

The girl with the bangs jumped in to talk about a scuba course she'd taken at a quarry outside of Boston. The girl in the striped top mentioned she'd been to Sydney.

"I've always wanted to go to Australia," Jamie put in. "They've got cassowaries, you know?" Cassowaries are giant birds that have this crazy sharp bone that grows out of their foreheads. Jamie couldn't imagine anything cooler or more ridiculous. Suddenly, everyone stopped talking and just stared blankly at Jamie. She blushed deeply.

"You can go topless on the beaches. Nobody cares," Ethan went on. Jamie gulped the last of her drink. She pictured hot girls with Australian accents and bare breasts bouncing around on the sand, maybe playing volleyball or . . . didn't they play cricket in Australia? Topless girls playing cricket with Ethan.

The conversation rolled along. Ethan mentioned how big the

Australian sharks are and how deadly the snakes are — all the stuff *they* would have talked about together, if they were still "together." Jamie tried to look enthused, but it was impossible. Ethan was supposed to be noticing how happy she was without him. But he wasn't noticing her much at all. And he seemed pretty happy himself.

Jamie picked at the rim of her empty cup, her stomach sinking. As the minutes ticked on, she felt more and more out of place. She needed another drink. In fact, she felt like she might need five drinks. She squeezed Ethan's arm and gave him an "I'll be back" look. She turned on her heel as if she had somewhere interesting to be and headed up the stairs.

"Beth," she gasped, relieved to see her cousin's friendly face behind the bar. "What are you doing up here?"

Beth grinned. "I'm the bartender, baby. What'll you have?"

"Two screwdrivers."

Beth nodded, even though she was clearly distracted. Still, she seemed to be in her element as she clutched a bottle in each hand and chatted with people to her left and right, all without missing a beat. "On the house," she said as she slipped Jamie two full cups, accepted the sloppy kiss Jamie laid on her cheek, and then turned to serve somebody else.

Wanting to loosen up before she went back downstairs, Jamie moved to the edge of the room and downed one of the screwdrivers, then started on the other. She watched the people who were dancing in the middle of the room. Slowly, her head started to feel lighter on her shoulders. The music was some kind of Caribbean dance stuff with steel drums, and it sounded nice. She was feeling better already.

"I brought this CD."

Jamie swiveled her head on her neck loosely to find Ethan's friend Scott standing to her left. He leaned against the wall beside her. "I love this stuff," he said.

Jamie felt much more relaxed now that she was away from Ethan. "You're dressed like a guy who would," she commented.

Scott was wearing a brightly colored Hawaiian shirt with a hula dancer on the pocket and baggy denim carpenter shorts.

"Yeah, well, my fashion sense and my music tastes are part of my charm," he said with a chuckle. "You need help with that drink?"

Jamie looked down at her half-empty cup, then smiled. "I could use some help getting another one." She fished an ice cube out of the mixture of vodka and OJ and stuck it in her mouth.

"You got it."

Scott disappeared for a few seconds, and then reappeared back at her side with the refill. "So, what brings you here tonight?"

"Ethan invited me."

"But didn't you guys break up?"

Jamie chomped on her ice and shrugged her shoulders. "We did. But we're trying to be all adultlike and put everything behind us."

"Wow, that's great. Isn't it awkward, though? Being here as his friend?"

"Nah, I'm perfectly okay with it." Jamie figured that maybe if she said things like this, it would get back to Ethan through Scott.

"Really?"

"Yeah. I mean, it was just a summer thing, you know?"

"Right, I hear that." Scott said, sort of implying that he'd been the victim of a similar kind of breakup before.

"I really love that shirt," Jamie giggled and tugged at one of Scott's middle buttons. She was so close to feeling okay. Scott and the screwdrivers made for a wonderful distraction.

"Thanks. I like your —" He looked her up and down, shyly. "Um, you look different. You look . . . amazing. Not that you didn't look . . . um . . . before."

Jamie was flattered by how flustered he was. It made her feel like she was a supermodel and all of a sudden she was brimming with confidence. "Let's dance." Jamie took a big gulp of her drink, grabbed his hand, and dragged him out onto the floor. She wondered what Ella's rule would be about flirting with Ethan's friends. Knowing her cousin, she'd probably consider it a good thing.

In the middle of the dance floor, Jamie started swaying, first her hips and then her whole body. She hoped Ethan would come upstairs any second and see her.

"You're not going scuba diving this summer, are you?" she asked Scott, trying to make some small talk.

Scott shook his head. "No, but my dad and I are flying to Myrtle Beach at the end of the summer."

"That sounds like so much fun."

"It's gonna be great. We're taking the Cessna."

"Your dad knows how to fly planes?"

"Yeah, so do I. Remember? We do that advertising business."

Jamie stared at him blankly, and gulped at her drink. Then it all started to come back to her — their first meeting at Ethan's. "Oh yeah, yeah. Sorry." She tucked her crazy hair behind her ears happily, then put her hands on Scott's shoulders, moving in close to him.

While she and Scott were dancing, Beth came by to ask if Jamie wanted to leave, but Jamie shooed her cousin away.

Thankfully, Scott was interesting. Jamie would have made conversation with a flagpole just to look like she had something to do, but Scott turned out to be way more entertaining than necessary. His father had been in the military and had lived all over the world — Germany, Italy, Spain. He and Jamie shouted about it over the music while her hands remained tightly on his shoulders. Pretty soon she decided she didn't care anymore whether Ethan saw her or not. After all, there were other boys to keep her occupied.

After a while, they were both covered in sweat and Jamie felt lighter than air. She felt powerful and sexy, and not at all nervous about it, like she'd been before.

"Do you want to go out back and sit on the deck?" Scott asked, fanning himself with his hands. "It's hot as hell in here."

"I have a better idea. Let's go down to the beach," she suggested, getting a sudden urge to dip her feet in the water and be far away and alone with Scott. "I'll get us some drinks."

Jamie led the way across the lawn. Once they got to the sand, Scott sat down and rested while Jamie kicked off her slides and ran down to the water, spilling half her drink along the way. She dipped her toes in once and then hurried back to where Scott was lounging. She flopped down onto her back. Her head was swimming in a sea of booze but she didn't care. She was dizzy, and better yet, happy. She felt like she could almost forget about Ethan completely.

"Are you feeling okay?" Scott asked.

"Never better."

"Can I get you a glass of water or anything?"

Jamie shook her head at the sky and lifted her neck to sip her drink. Her head felt floppy on her neck.

They stayed there, silent, for several minutes. Jamie tried counting stars, but they all started to cross and blend together into this one giant light.

"Ethan was such an asshole to you," Scott said finally. "He kept saying he was gonna break up with you, but he just kept stringing you along."

Jamie turned her head, which made her dizzier. She wanted to rub at her nose because it itched, but her aim was completely off, so she ended up poking her eye. After she regained her focus, she looked directly at Scott. "Why are we talking about Ethan?"

"I don't know. You just seem kind of . . . upset. . . ."

Jamie laughed, but it didn't even sound like her laugh, and that made her want to laugh more. "What do you mean? I'm great." The last word came out as two high-pitched syllables.

"Let's just say you don't seem like the kind of girl who drags strange guys out onto the beach at night."

Jamie rolled onto her side and grinned at him. "You're only a little strange." She slipped a hand under his shirt, touching his chest and feeling the thrum of his heartbeat under his surprisingly soft skin.

Scott shifted uncomfortably. He swallowed so loudly that Jamie could hear it, and then he cleared his throat. If Jamie hadn't been touching him, she would have taken it as a signal to back off.

But the rhythm under his ribs told her that Scott actually liked what she was doing.

A warm pleasant feeling spread through Jamie's body. She slid her hand along Scott's side, down to his hipbone, feeling the line of his boxers through his shorts and remembering Ethan. Scott watched her hand, then moved his fingers down to hers, pushing them away, even though it seemed as if that was the last thing he wanted to do. She kissed the side of his lips, putting her hands to his face and turning it so that his lips were on hers. They kissed. Jamie smiled and tilted her head, deepening the kiss. She started pulling down the straps of her tank top.

Suddenly, Scott drew back. "Jamie. I think we should stop."

But she didn't listen. She started kissing him again, forcefully, and kept tugging down her straps. Then Scott reached out to touch her.

Instead of stroking her skin, though, he pulled her straps up.

"Jamie, please. I — we — shouldn't be doing this. I want to, but it's a bad idea."

Scott stood up rather quickly and yanked her up onto her feet so fast that Jamie's head wobbled. "You're just not like this," he told her flatly.

Jamie scowled at Scott's flushed face. Suddenly, she felt naked and exposed. She crossed her arms over her chest.

"Like what?"

"I'm sorry, I just know this isn't right. You're so sexy, Jamie, and beautiful but . . . when you're sober, we can . . . ."

All Jamie heard was the rejection. She could feel the blood rushing to her toes and fingers and face. Why the hell couldn't anything go right for her? Guys were always chasing girls for sex, and here she was, offering it up. Was she that repulsive?

Scott was still talking, but none of it mattered to Jamie. He was saying if he didn't think she were so cool, he wouldn't care about some meaningless hookup, and something about maybe if she really got over Ethan, etc., etc. That did it. Before she knew what she was doing, she'd moved right up to him and slapped him hard across the face. Instantly, she wished she could take it back. But it was too late. Scott jerked back, his cheek bright red from the imprint of her hand and his eyes wide in disbelief.

Jamie watched him, tears trembling on her lower lids. She was too ashamed to apologize. Or maybe she was too drunk. Her head was whirling. The only thing she wanted to do was get away. She pivoted, ready to take off toward the house, but then stopped in her tracks. Only a few feet across the grass, Ethan stood frozen, staring at her, then at Scott, then at her again. His hands were resting on his perfect hip bones. He looked totally sober, and speechless.

"Jamie," Ethan finally said. "Maybe it's time for you to go home."

They didn't speak a word on the short ride home. When they arrived at her cottage, Ethan opened the passenger side door for Jamie and she slipped out of her seat silently.

Ethan started back toward his side of the car. He was just going to leave. Jamie could feel her bottom lip trembling. She felt terrible for what she'd done. No wonder he'd kicked her out of the party.

"I'm so sorry, Ethan," she whispered.

He shook his head. "Whatever. I gotta get back."

Jamie swallowed and pursed her lips. She'd never win him back now. In fact, she'd probably never see him again. And it was all her fault.

Without another word, he got into the car. His tires peeled out on the gravel before the car disappeared into a blaze of taillights.

Jamie stood watching for several seconds, unable to process just how big a fool she'd made of herself. Finally, she started toward her cottage. She was almost to her door when she realized there were voices coming from Uncle Gary's yard. She stepped back, then walked over to get a closer look. George and Cara were sitting on the picnic table in the moonlight, holding hands.

They waved Jamie over. Jamie scowled at them. She couldn't find any other facial expression in her repertoire at the moment. Plus, she hated the fact that George, of all people, had managed to find love while she was miserable. But she started to walk over, anyway.

She'd only taken two steps forward when she stumbled a little.

"Are you okay?" George asked, getting halfway up from his seat. Jamie waved her arms to indicate she wanted him to stay where he was. She wanted to at least carry herself to the table with some grace. She opened her mouth to say something along those lines. But when she tried, she doubled over and puked instead.

15

Ella flipped over in her bed for the millionth time and looked at the clock — 2:37 A.M. She wished the cottage had air-conditioning. Then she could crawl under her covers and hibernate. The Egyptian cotton sheets she'd bought at Crate and Barrel were sticking to her, which Ella thought was ironic, considering how damn hot it probably was in Egypt and how Egyptians should know better than to make sticky sheets.

In the next bed, Kelsi snored lightly. She'd gotten home around midnight, her eyes sparkling and her cheeks rosy. She'd also only vaguely answered the pointed questions Ella had asked about where she and Peter had gone, what they'd done. All Kelsi said was, "Nothing exciting. We just hung out. I'm going to bed." Ella seethed — she had come home early from her own date just to give Kelsi a proper interrogation. The guy from Ahoy had turned out to be boring and self-absorbed anyway, and wasn't all that cute the second time around.

Now Ella was left to wonder why Kelsi was sleeping so

soundly. What had made her so tired? Was it hours of unbridled, passionate sex with Peter? Ever since yesterday, when Kelsi had bought the lingerie downtown, Ella couldn't stop obsessing over it.

"Damn it," she whispered, switching onto her side. She wished she'd gone to the party with her cousins tonight instead. Then maybe she'd be tired out from dancing and could actually fall asleep. It seemed that the perfect, comfortable position was just beyond her grasp. She tried to imagine Peter lying beside her in bed. His arms were around her waist, his front was pressed into her back. Their bodies were melded together. Then she felt that he was turned on.

She rolled over and they started kissing, and then both their clothes were off. But when Ella opened her eyes, she realized just how wide awake and alone she was. She began to readjust her covers when she heard a rustling out in the grass.

It's nothing. Maybe a heron walking up from the ocean. She just needed to relax. She laid back and rolled to her other side, but just as she got settled, she heard the sound again, only louder, and closer.

It was definite this time. Someone was outside.

Ella got out of bed slowly, not wanting to wake Kelsi, and peered out the window. Nothing. The thin camisole she wore barely covered her, and she shivered, suddenly feeling chilled. She pressed the tip of her nose to the screen and shielded her eyes, blocking out the light of the moon.

"Kelsi."

Ella jumped, her heart pounded relentlessly before the voice registered. She moved her face closer to the screen.

"Peter," she whispered.

"Ella?"

She moved her finger in front of her lips. "Shh, hold on."

Ella looked back over her shoulder and listened for a moment. Kelsi was still snoring delicately. Then she tiptoed backward from the window and felt along the floor with her bare feet for piles of clothes. Finally, she bent down and sifted what felt like her Juicy shorts out of a pile. In the hallway, she pulled the shorts on over her undies. Holding her breath, she quietly walked down the hall and sidled up to the door that led to the back deck, then slid the lock open as gently as she could. Ella paused, listening to the calmness inside the house. Nothing, and no one, was stirring. She cracked open the door and listened again, then slid out into the night.

Peter was already standing at the foot of the porch stairs, his white T-shirt reflecting the glow of the moon.

"Over here," Ella whispered, motioning him farther out into the grass. They stopped at a maple tree halfway across the lawn, and Peter pulled out a pack of trusty Marlboros. Ella realized she was still holding her breath, so she let it out in a short burst and took one of the cigarettes.

"What's going on?" she asked, resting one hand against the bark of the tree.

"Kelsi told me to come wake her up."

"Oh." Ella's voice came out all crackly, like her jealousy was piercing her vocal chords. She put the cigarette in her mouth and Peter lit it for her.

"Looks like I got you instead." He put one hand against the tree, too, so that they were face-to-face. All of a sudden, Peter seemed much taller than she was. The way he smelled made Ella think of a night in the Mediterranean, under olive trees. She avoided his eyes and tried not to show her excitement. She'd never felt so nervous with a boy in her life.

"I can go and get her. . . ." Ella said, backing up a little to give herself some space and catch her breath.

Peter stopped her with a hand on her waist. His touch was as light as a butterfly.

"That's okay."

They stood there motionless for a minute and just took each other in.

"Have you played any gigs lately?" Ella asked, skimming his face quickly with her eyes. She couldn't think of anything else to say.

"Not lately."

"Oh." More silence. "Well, how're things at the diner?"

Peter let out a long sigh through closed lips. "Same shit, different day, you know?"

Ella picked some bark off the tree. What was wrong with her? Who cared about the diner? Here she was, where she'd wanted to be all summer long. In fact, she'd had more than one fantasy in which Peter showed up at her window in the middle of the night. But in her dreams, she was more bold, like the usual Ella. Now she finally had the chance to do something, but she kept thinking about Kelsi sleeping peacefully back at the house. She felt so guilty, she started to tremble.

"Are you cold?" Peter reached out and rubbed her left arm, just above the elbow.

"I'm fine. It's just this night breeze — I get the chills very easily."

He was silent as his hand kept stroking her arm. She wanted him to, and she didn't want him to.

It gave her that same feeling she'd gotten in the car. Like her body had a mind of its own.

"Well, I'll tell Kelsi you stopped by," she said at last.

She couldn't believe she was doing it, but she was extricating herself from his gentle touch. She was backing away. She dropped the cigarette on the ground and stamped it out.

He uttered one word — "Wait" — but Ella ignored it.

She retreated a few feet across the grass, and then turned toward the deck, her pulse racing. She was a mixture of desire and guilt and bitter disappointment. She bit her lip so hard, she actually made it bleed a little.

At the bottom of the stairs she swiveled around to take one last look at Peter. If he was at all surprised at the turn of events, he didn't show it. He just stood there carelessly, watching her silhouette. Ella thought she saw him shrug his shoulders, just a little bit. Then he turned, and walked away.

16

Sometime in the middle of the night, Beth woke up with the eerie feeling that someone was watching her. She rolled far enough over in bed to see the illuminated outline of her bedroom door. It looked like it was cracked open. She knew she'd closed it. And then something shifted at the foot of the bed.

"Shit!" Beth gasped.

She shrank back against the headboard, making out the figure in the bright moonlight sifting through the window. It was George, sitting on the edge of the mattress, one hand in front of his face, shushing her, and the other beside her knee. Beth's heart was beating a mile a minute. "Jesus, George, you scared me."

"I was trying to figure out whether I should wake you," he whispered.

Beth rubbed her forehead, trying to orient herself. The glowing red numbers of the clock said it was 3:13 A.M. She'd gone to bed right after they'd gotten home from the party, around 1:00. What was George doing in her room two hours later?

She swallowed as she stretched out her legs again. Her skin felt hot. George crawled up to her left side and lay on his stomach, resting his upper body on his elbows.

In the darkness, Beth could see his outline and the glint of his eyes, but not much else. Even in the pitch-black darkness, he was adorable.

"What's up?" she asked, calmer now.

George ran both his hands through his hair and let out a deep, resigned sigh. "I don't know."

The way he said it was serious. Beth felt paralyzed. There was something big happening here. George was lying on her bed. It was dark. It was the middle of the night. There wasn't the usual "old pal" comfortability between them anymore. There was a tension so palpable it felt heavy.

"Weren't you hanging out with Cara?"

"She went home. It's not . . . it doesn't matter." George picked at some invisible lint on the blanket covering the parts of Beth that were covered. "I came up here because I just had to talk to you. . . ." He sidled over to get a little closer to her.

Beth swallowed. "About what?" Her head was throbbing, and she knew it wasn't a symptom of a hangover. She had the dawning suspicion that things were about to change between them forever.

"We've been friends for a long time. . . ."

She tugged the blanket up against her chest. What was she going to do if he tried to kiss her? All she knew was that she had the urge to touch his face, his neck. He seemed to have taken on some different aura. Suddenly, George was somebody she didn't completely know.

"You mean a lot to me, you know that?" he said.

Beth nodded. George cleared his throat and went on.

"And I've never had a girlfriend. I mean, I don't want things to change between us."

"Sure, I understand," Beth agreed, hypnotized. The word *girlfriend* practically gave her an electric shock.

With a jerk, George straightened up and pulled his legs in so he was sitting Indian style. Beth sat up, too, her face floating close to his.

"So I just wanted to tell you that. Well, it's probably obvious." He looked down at the bedspread. "Cara and I kinda hooked up tonight. I mean, I guess we're a *thing* now."

"Oh." *Oh.*

Whatever big feeling that had been growing in Beth shrank down to the size of a flea in the matter of an instant. Beth felt herself deflating, getting smaller and smaller.

"Anyway, it's a big milestone for me, so I just had to tell you right away," George finished.

Beth straightened up against the headboard. They were silent for several seconds. George seemed to have run out of words.

"Well," Beth said, trying to sound casual. But then a hard kernel of anger poked her in the stomach. "Why couldn't this wait until tomorrow?"

"Um, because you're my best friend, and I wanted to make sure it was . . . okay with you."

Beth gritted her teeth. "Why wouldn't it be okay?"

"I don't know. I just didn't know if . . ." George sounded lost, but she wasn't going to reel him in. If he had something to say, he needed to just say it. "I just wanted to make sure you were cool with it, I guess."

"Why wouldn't I be cool with it?" Beth knew she sounded bitchy. She couldn't stop herself. "I'm cool with anything at 3 A.M., except being woken up."

"I'm sorry. . . ."

"George, I'm really tired. If you wanna go elope to Vegas with Cara, that's great with me. I'm happy for you. Really. It's about time because you're a great guy." She hated herself for saying the last part because she knew he really was and she knew she didn't sound like she meant it. "Just . . . can you let me sleep?"

"Yeah," George nervously retreated across the bed and Beth rolled over onto her stomach. "Good night, Bethy." She felt his body move away, and leave the bed.

She could hear him walking to the door, and then felt him hovering. She knew he was standing there, trying to figure out a way to fix whatever he'd done wrong. After a few seconds, her door squeaked closed and then Beth could hear the low click of George's own door shutting behind him.

Beth rolled onto her back. She balled her hands into fists and slammed them against the mattress about ten times.

How had this happened? She felt consumed with hurt and jealousy. But why? Was she, like, in love with George or something? Jesus. What if she was? It was too late to do anything about it.

And it was too ludicrous to even be funny.

Beth's eyes started filling up with tears. She swallowed and clamped her jaw tight. Beth wasn't an emotional girl. She was physical. So she grabbed her pillow and tried to choke the life out of two fistfuls of fabric before going slack and blank.

She wasn't going to let anyone, not even Chauncy the cork fisherman, see her cry over George.

17

Most people would have Ella pegged for a roller-coaster kind of girl, but really she loved the Ferris wheel. It was the view from the top that excited her. From Funville, U.S.A., which was slightly inland, you could see just the hint of the ocean, and the sweep of the town in between. Ella and her youngest cousin, Jessi, sat stopped at the second-highest spot, staring down at the twinkling orange lights just beginning to pop in the dusk. Ella felt a breeze on her neck and wondered about rain. There was supposed to be a storm on its way, but she hadn't seen any sign of it yet.

"We gotta go to the haunted house," Jessi said cheerfully as she peered over the other side of their basket and pointed at all the rides. Ella followed her gaze. The park was small, so it was easy to pick out the haunted house, the merry-go-round, and the pirate ship among other rides. There were two old-school-style wooden roller coasters along the outer rim — miniversions of the ones you see at real theme parks. A group of riders was beginning the descent down one of the dips, with a collective scream that could be heard for miles.

"You almost peed your pants the last time we went, remember?" Ella said.

Jessi got perturbed. "I'm much older now."

"Whatever you say, Jess."

Ella bit back a smile. It was already the end of July. In another two weeks or so, Ella and Kelsi would be heading home. And by that time, Jessi might feel as if she had grown up even more.

They were the last pair of their group to get off the ride. Kelsi, Peter, and the two other little cousins, Drew and Jordan, were waiting for them by the white metal exit gate.

"These guys want to ride on the go-karts," Kelsi said, holding Drew and Jordan by their hands. Ella stole a glance at Peter. He hadn't looked at her the few times she'd seen him since the night behind the cottage, and he didn't look at her now. Ella had already decided not to let it bother her. But her chest pinched a little. She wouldn't even have come tonight if the kids hadn't roped her into it.

She put on a smile for Jessi. "How 'bout it, Jess? Can the haunted house wait?" Jessi nodded eagerly as she pulled Ella down the path that led to the go-karts.

"Actually, would you mind taking them for a while on your own?" Kelsi asked Ella. "Peter's hungry. I think we'll go get some fries or something and sit this one out, if that's okay."

"Um, okay." Ella couldn't think of a reason why not. The park was small and easy to find people in. Drew and Jordan let go of Kelsi and ran to catch up with Ella, who let them drag her away.

Ella consoled herself by thinking that at least Peter and Kelsi couldn't exactly go off and have sex in Funville, U.S.A., unless they found a secluded corner in the fun house. She freed her hand

116

from Drew's and brushed her bangs out of her eyes. She supposed anything was possible.

On line for the go-karts, Jessi pulled Ella's arms around her. Jordan tugged at her elbows. "Ella, I want you to hug me, too." Drew kept slapping his arms until Ella finally dug out some bug spray from her bag. What was it about little kids and mosquitoes?

They rode the go-karts three times. Then they walked to the closest roller coaster and waited on line for twenty minutes for a ride that jerked Ella around until her neck hurt. They went to the second coaster and waited for thirty minutes. From the top of a high curve, Ella thought she glimpsed Peter and Kelsi on the ground, waiting outside the Himalayan, but when they walked by it a few minutes later, they were gone.

The next path they took led them to the farthest back corner of Funville. The haunted house — which was actually more like a trailer — stood ahead of them in the distance, against a fence that bordered an empty field. It should have *loomed* ahead of them, but it was not that scary. It was covered with an array of poorly painted demons and a terrified, big-breasted woman that Kelsi had said was "misogynistic," whatever that meant.

Reluctantly, Ella got on line. The kids were squeezing her hands hard now.

"If you guys keep doing that, I'm gonna lose my circulation and have to get my arms amputated," Ella warned.

When they made their way through the slow-moving line, a man dressed as the grim reaper emerged through a hinged, black door. He told them to "Enter at your own risk," in a voice that was meant to be menacing, but instead was squeaky-sounding, kind of like SpongeBob SquarePants instead of the devil.

The first hall was completely black. Ella confidently felt her way along, knowing the way almost by heart, the kids clinging to her waist and her hands. They wandered through a collection of black-lit gravestones made of Styrofoam, then a lab full of experiments in beakers, fake-looking eyeballs, and plastic hands. The obligatory mad scientist laughed maniacally.

It was a combination of the fakeness of it all and the fact that there were cracks in the walls where you could see the cords and pulleys that made the whole thing more funny than scary. By the time Ella reached the bridge, which was her favorite part, the kids had run far ahead of her, eager to see what was next.

The bridge crossed only a couple of feet above the ground, but the spinning neon lights underneath it gave you the illusion that you were dangling thousands of feet up in space. At the other end, Ella could see a figure, and the hairs on the back of her neck stood up. It was dark, but she could have made him out anywhere. Where had he come from? And where was Kelsi? He was holding his hands out to the side like Ella sometimes did, like a trapeze artist, to heighten the feeling of floating. Watching him, her chest throbbed.

Her feet took her two steps backward. She would turn around. Kelsi was probably outside, waiting. Ella should go outside and wait with her.

But something in her caved. She padded across the bridge, shaking. She paused within inches of his outstretched hand, then moved forward slightly, so that his fingers brushed her collarbone.

Peter turned to look at her. Without a word, he reached down to grab her waist, his fingers pressing into the skin underneath her shirt. Ella smiled, and he gave her a half-amused grin. He gently pushed her against the railing of the bridge. Ella raised her eyes to look at him, and he instantly caught her mouth with his. His stubble rubbed the top of Ella's lips. His tongue tasted of smoke and salt. He was delicious. Ella kissed back, hard, pressing close to him. She felt like melting into oblivion and never coming back to Earth.

His hands traveled down from her waist to her behind. He pulled her in even closer, kissing her with such hunger that it was almost frightening. Ella kept her eyes open, watching his face while his eyes were closed, as if he was having a wonderful dream.

Then she realized she wasn't melting at all. With the lights spinning around them, she felt like an astronaut, cut loose from the shuttle and drifting into space.

18

"Look, Paul Bunyan. I didn't ask you to chop anything down."

Beth watched George backing down the beach with some wood he had found for his birthday bonfire. He pulled it up to the pile Beth had already made, not turning to look at her until he'd laid it down. It looked like he had killed an entire a tree.

George smiled proudly. "I didn't chop it down. I found it. Who's the man?"

"George," Beth said, tapping at the log with her toe. "There's no way we're gonna be able to get this onto the fire. It's too big. We'd need to chop it up with an ax or something. You don't have an ax on you, do you?"

George scowled. "You just can't accept that I have a big one."

"Oh, puh-lease. You can be so freaking gross."

"I say it's fine. My work here is done." He brushed his hands together in an "all finished" gesture. "Deal with it, Beth. I've got a big one for you."

"You are so sick." Beth didn't laugh. She didn't even smile. In fact, she could hardly look at George. Why was he getting such a kick out of teasing her that way? "Anyway, it looks soggy."

George studied her for a second, his hands on his waist. He was wearing a bright orange T-shirt and black shorts. Beth concentrated on his clothes. She couldn't bring herself to look him in the eyes.

"It's been raining for a week," he said. "Everything's soggy."

Beth just rolled her eyes. George shrugged his shoulders in confusion, then disappeared back into the brush for more wood.

When he came out again, he was carrying two normal-size pieces. He dropped them by the pile. "Good enough?"

Good enough? It was *his* birthday bonfire. Beth had gotten the permit to have the fire on the beach. She'd gotten Ella to get them beer with her fake ID. She'd made all the cousins swear up and down they were coming. And George was acting as if picking up two logs required some kind of Herculean effort.

She had to bite her tongue or risk getting into a fight. But she just couldn't resist. "I'm sorry, George. Are my pesky birthday plans getting in the way of your *other* festivities?"

"There are no *other* festivities." George shifted from one foot to the other.

"Right." Beth wanted to say something about the festivities being in Cara's pants, but this time she held back. "You know, you're leaving in two days and I thought you might not mind spending time with me."

"I don't mind spending time with you."

"That's big of you," she spat out, before she could stop herself. Since the night George had come into her room, she was still feeling very small inside. She hated that she couldn't shake that emotion. She was used to being open and honest with George.

Lately, Beth had tried to avoid hanging out with George and Cara. It seemed he wanted Beth to do everything with them. When they went downtown for ice cream, he begged her to come. He wanted her to give Cara surfing pointers because he said Beth was a better teacher than he was. He didn't seem to get the hint when she kept making excuses.

George let out a sigh, then walked off into the brush yet again. Beth sank onto her knees in the sand and started organizing the wood and kindling. She glanced at the sky, hoping the clouds would pass. Mostly because something *had* to go right. The fact that rain looked inevitable seemed to prove that the dark forces of the universe were conspiring against her.

"Want me to get more?" George said, coming to the edge of the pit with an armful of kindling.

"No, that's fine," she said, contrite. "That's really great." He watched as she arranged and rearranged the kindling. Then he knelt beside her and tried to help, reaching out his hand for her to hand him some wood.

Beth glanced at the familiar scar on his palm. As a joke one night, after watching *Stand By Me* on HBO, they'd decided to become blood brother and sister. Beth had sworn up and down that if George cut his hand she would, too. Of course, some of their silliness that night could be attributed to the fact that they'd been drinking George's stepdad's Smirnoff Ices — almost an entire case worth.

George had sliced his hand, just near the thumb, with a paring

122

knife from the kitchen, but when it came time for Beth to do it, she couldn't go through with it.

George hadn't pushed it like Beth would have if the situation were reversed. He'd nodded and said it was okay. He bit his lip while his hand throbbed and Beth was nice enough to put a Band-Aid on the cut. He'd never brought it up again.

Now, remembering, Beth felt evil for treating him so badly. George was always so good to her, which may have been why she felt so tormented by him now.

"So, are you and Cara gonna keep in touch?" she asked, putting all the kindness she could muster into her voice.

George nodded. "Yeah, I think so. I guess we'll e-mail and maybe try to visit each other. I mean, we haven't really talked about it."

Why was this stuff so difficult for Beth to hear?

"It's more the 'right now' I'm worried about," he said, sinking deeper onto his knees and clasping his hands.

"What do you mean?" Beth had picked up a stick and was cracking it into little pieces. What could happen in two days?

"Well, we've, you know, fooled around. Kissed or whatever. But I think she probably expects more." George's face was beet-red.

Beth fought the urge to clear her throat. "And that's a bad thing?" She was trying really hard to sound like a supportive friend.

"No, no. Definitely not. But, I'm just — well — you know." He looked up at Beth from under his eyebrows, shyly. Beth knew, of course, that George — like her — was a virgin. But she wasn't going to help him out here. "I don't want us to end the summer without, you know, me showing her I'm . . . uh, up for it. I don't want to go into a long-distance relationship like that."

"I thought you said you hadn't discussed that."

"We haven't." George stared at the ground.

Beth searched her mind for the most well-intentioned thing she could think of to say. It was a stretch. "Well, you know, you're probably fine. You don't have to pretend you're more experienced than you are, I don't think. You can just, maybe, let her take the lead?" She was proud of herself for standing by George and giving him advice.

He shook his head. "You don't understand, Beth. If you were with someone you'd want *him* to take the lead."

"I don't know. . . ."

"Well, that's the thing. You don't get it." George sighed and stood up.

"Wait, wait, wait. I don't get it?" Beth stood up, too, trying to quench the burning starting at the bottom of her throat. "What do you mean?"

"I don't know," he said in a confused tone. "You just haven't, you know, had sex or anything yet. Really."

"I've been closer than you have," Beth countered, her stomach trembling wildly. She knew that probably wasn't really true.

George realized that he'd hit a nerve. He was silent for a moment. "You're right. Never mind."

But Beth couldn't let it go. She felt all the hurt welling up in her at once. It was like a freight train that would run right over what they were saying to each other. "Wait, how did I all of a sudden become the person who 'doesn't get it'?"

George tried to backtrack. "Forget it. I don't know what I'm talking about."

"Maybe *you* don't get it."

George half laughed. "Get what?"

Beth searched the air above her head for an answer. "I don't know. Maybe you don't see that you're just Cara's . . . *summer boy.* It's not going to last, George. You're talking about the long-distance thing, blah blah blah. You're making all these plans. Do you really think she's interested? You're, like, her little fling. I don't see why you're making it into this huge romance when it's obvious to everyone but you that it's not."

George's face had gone from flushed to pale. He clenched his jaw tight. As soon as the words were out of Beth's mouth, she wished she could take them back.

"You're probably right. I never said it was this big serious thing."

Beth stared at him. He looked like a deer caught in the head-lights of an enormous SUV. She wanted to say she was sorry, but she just couldn't.

"I'm done with making this fire," he said. "I'm going back to the house." His face became familiar again, but still distant. Like the George she knew had taken on a different form. In all the time she'd known him, Beth had never seen him really angry with her.

"Okay," Beth whispered.

She pretended to be busy as he walked back down the beach.

She knew she'd been wrong to yell at him. She was probably wrong about Cara. They could end up married for all Beth knew. But she was still afraid that she was losing him.

Then it occurred to her that maybe she already had.

125

19

Regis and Kelly were interviewing Nicolas Cage. It seemed to Jamie that Regis and Kelly were always interviewing Nicolas Cage. She reached down to the floor and picked up her coffee mug, taking a long gulp as she stared at the TV screen. After Ethan's disastrous party and her getting sick, she'd holed up inside again, hiding from the world. The phone rang.

"Mom," she said into the receiver, seeing the number on the caller ID. These days the phone was wherever Jamie was, just in case Ethan might call again.

"Jamie, I'm afraid I can't make it up this week," her mom said, sounding extremely apologetic. "There's a crisis at work and . . ."

"I'm fine. Don't worry about it." Jamie shifted around so that her feet touched the floor, knocking over a bag of Tostitos. The floor surrounding the couch was a minefield of snack bags and coffee mugs.

"I just can't stop thinking about what a jerk he was."

"Mom, Ethan's not a jerk."

"I don't want you to talk to him anymore, Jamie."

"Don't worry. He went to that writer's workshop. I don't even know if he's coming back."

"Well, if he does call, I want you to hang up on him."

"We're just about to leave for the beach." Jamie picked up the remote. "Talk to you later?"

After she'd hung up, she turned up the volume on the TV and grabbed a doughnut from the nearly empty box on the coffee table. Lying back on the couch, she flipped through the channels and finally settled on a documentary about death rituals in Thailand. A bunch of people were standing on the edge of a body of water, tossing petals at a floating coffin. Bored and restless, Jamie fiddled with her locket mindlessly, and then opened it and stared at the picture inside.

The picture had been taken when Jamie was nine. In it, her black hair was even curlier and wilder than it was now, and hung all the way down to her butt. She was dressed in short shorts and a pink tank top, perched on the front stoop of their old house. Her hands hung at her sides, her belly poked out, and her arms and legs were as skinny as twigs. Her eyes were gently tilted like a cat's.

There was something reserved about the girl Jamie had been. But she'd also been happy. The look on her face was something so unfamiliar — she was inquisitive, optimistic, innocent, and blissfully naive.

I'm nothing like that anymore, Jamie thought. She felt like throwing petals at herself.

Oh God. She sat up, shaking out her ratty, unwashed hair. Ella had been right that day in her room. Jamie *was* falling into a void. She had to get out.

She stood up and headed for the back door, grabbing her cotton sun hat from its peg and walking out into the yard, then down to the water. George's birthday bonfire wouldn't be until that night, so she had lots of time to kill.

There was a border of rocks between the lawn and the shore and Jamie carefully picked her way around the barnacles, stepping onto the sand uncovered by low tide. At this time of day, the ocean that usually backed up to the house was more like a shallow lagoon — a finger of water cutting through the marsh and the dunes.

Jamie didn't know she was planning to wade in until she'd taken the first couple of steps. The water was so shallow and clear, she could see the hermit crabs dotting the sand underneath. Each time she bent to pick up one, its eyes and claws disappeared into its shell. She dropped one, then another, behind her, and moved deeper into the water, wading up to her thighs, just below the hem of her overalls. That was as deep as the water went. It then sloped up to the shore across the way.

Jamie followed the slope, emerging on the other side and picking up her pace. It felt like her legs could carry her on forever if they wanted to, without consulting any other part of her body for permission.

The shore petered off into a collection of dunes, dotted with patches of sea grass. It was all private property, but Jamie trudged through them, anyway. She made it so far into the dunes that when she did a 360, she couldn't see any houses anywhere. She wondered what it would be like to yell at the top of her lungs.

When she emerged on a new stretch of beach, she kept walking. Eventually, sea grass became houses — a Spanish-style terra-cotta villa, two ranches. And finally, Ethan's house.

She climbed the stairs of the deck and cupped her hands against the glass, staring in. The house was empty and immaculate. She knew Ethan was away for the writing course, but his parents were probably still in town. She walked back to the railing, leaned on it, and stared out at the water, thinking. Then she walked over to the Weber grill and knelt beside it, feeling underneath for the magnetic compartment. She slid it open, and pulled out the silver key inside, feeling strangely calm.

When she cracked open the door, its echo bounced back at her. She wiped her feet on the mat before stepping inside, her heart pounding in her ears. *I'm a stalker.* She carefully closed the door behind her and walked upstairs.

Ethan's room was sparse — a single bed with a plain off-white comforter, a metal bookshelf he'd put together himself. His books lay all over the place, facedown and pages open, dog-eared and stacked in random piles.

Jamie sat down on his bed gently, as if it might collapse underneath her. She lay back, listened to the sounds of the empty house and then, relaxing, pulled the covers around her. They still smelled faintly like Ethan. She lay there for several minutes, letting herself hurt. And then she pushed herself out of bed. Being here was worse than lying around at home. She walked back into the hallway and down to the kitchen, then down to the den.

The Millennium Falcon was in its usual spot on the table. Jamie slid onto the couch and stared at it. It stared back at her.

"What are you looking at?" she asked darkly.

Jamie nibbled on her pinky. She leaned toward it, picked it up and held it in her hands. She studied the places where tiny dots of clear glue stuck everything together. There must have been hundreds of miniature plastic parts, all connected intricately to make the final product. It was beautiful. She was mesmerized by the thought and effort that had obviously gone into it — she could see the places where he must have had to use tweezers to put the pieces together.

She put her finger on the little door on the left side. And then she pulled it off.

Wow, that felt good, she thought.

She stood up, pulling the pieces off one by one, gently at first, and then carelessly. Using both hands, she snapped the bridge in half. She crunched up the pieces in her fingers. The rest she dropped onto the floor. She didn't even realize she was crying until she looked down at the blurry mess at her feet. *Shit.* She let out a small moan, and swooped down to gather up the pieces. She dumped the splinters in handfuls onto the coffee table, then ran upstairs to the kitchen. Everybody had glue. Every family in the world had glue.

It was stupid, of course. Glue wouldn't do any good. She looked through two drawers, then gave up, walking back downstairs and sinking onto the couch.

"I'm such a psycho," she said out loud. She was mortified, as if Ethan and his family were standing there watching her have her breakdown.

She frantically tried to find a way out of this situation. What if she just took the pieces? That way, he'd think he'd taken it home, or that it had been misplaced, or something. No, he'd know exactly where he'd left it, wouldn't he? But at least he wouldn't see what she'd done.

She just had to fix it. She cast her eyes about the den. Maybe he still had the box it came in. Maybe it had instructions.

She ran back upstairs to his room and whipped his closet door open. Then she got on her knees and swung an arm under his bed. Her hand slapped against a cardboard box and she pulled it out. It wasn't the box for the kit. It was a box of Ethan's writings. Jamie leaned forward on her knees, lifting out a handful of paper. She was still sniffling. She rubbed at her nose with her arm and separated the top sheet from the pile, reading it.

What can be said?
The great arboreal oak is dead.
Behind my house it fell today
And more I cannot say
Because I'm lost in apathy, and you in ignominy.
I do not care for thee, my memory of tree.

Jamie remembered this one. Ethan had shown it to her last summer with particular pride, and she'd been impressed with the big words, which she would never have used in her own poetry. She scratched at her runny nose. Somehow, the poem seemed kind of stupid right now. Pretentious.

She sifted through the papers, pulling out another she remembered, one that was about her. She'd been sitting on Ethan's deck, drinking lemonade and drawing the ocean when he'd written it. Jamie remembered feeling so flattered.

> She leans back, a goddess drinking nectar
> Aphrodite or maybe Demeter
> Sketching summer on her palette
> The nectar summer on her palate
> Her hair a mass of sea grass
> And Poseidon in her eyes

Jamie started flipping through the poems more quickly, the disaster downstairs momentarily forgotten. Not one of Ethan's poems failed to include either Greek mythology or words like *arboreal*. Jamie had never noticed before how overblown it came across.

Finally, she laid the papers down, confused. Carefully, she tucked everything back into its place and slid the box under the bed. She stood up and drifted away, ghostlike.

At the top of the den stairs, she paused. She could still go down and pick up the pieces of the destroyed model. She could just make the whole thing disappear, and maybe Ethan would never suspect her of being the one who'd made it happen.

But she turned back into the kitchen instead.

Silently, she slipped out the back door, leaving the mess where it lay.

20

Ella stood in front of the mirror, pumping the applicator of her mascara in and out of the tube. She never went to a bonfire without mascara. It made her eyes stand out in the dark. Finally, she got enough on the wand to coat the lashes of both eyes. She leaned back and studied herself, smiling.

She'd gone through four outfits so far. As frustrating as it was to change so many times, she felt a little charge at thinking she was dressing for Peter. Pulling the clothes off, tugging them on, all with his face on her mind, made her feel sexy. Now she stood in just the cranberry strapless demi-bra and a pair of short shorts, admiring her body. She didn't know why she was wearing the new lingerie, except that she was riding a wave since what had happened at the park, and the wave required her to wear sultry stuff.

After putting on the black halter top she'd finally decided on, she walked out into the hall. "Kels?"

Her sister hadn't even started getting ready yet and the bonfire began in five minutes. PMS was a definite possibility. It was one of

Kelsi's few imperfections — she got it bad. Maybe she wouldn't go to the party at all. *That would be a blessing,* Ella thought. It had been misery being around Kelsi all week, ever since what had happened at the haunted house.

Every night since Peter and she had shared their taboo kiss, whenever Ella was lying in her bed, Peter occupied her mind as a separate entity from Kelsi — like there were no strings attached. He just seemed so right for Ella, so *meant* for her.

But, in the daylight, when Ella looked at Kelsi, she felt different. The guilty knowledge that she'd betrayed her sister was weighing heavily on her. She hadn't been sleeping. She'd hardly been eating. Her body temperature ran in hot and cold waves. But she knew if she had the chance to kiss Peter again, she'd do it in a heartbeat.

She walked toward the other end of the house, into the kitchen. Kelsi was there, sitting on a chair against the wall, talking on the phone, looking down at her feet. She was rolling her toes against the hardwood floor, saying "No," "Uh-huh," and "Yes," solemnly.

Ella poked her head into the living room, where her father was reading the newspaper. "Who's she talking to?" she asked.

He shrugged, looking uncomfortable. Ella knew that whenever there was drama involving either of his daughters, he tended to check out.

Ella listened to Kelsi's voice echoing down the hall. "I can't say over the phone. . . ." Kelsi whispered. The chair squeaked as it was pushed across the linoleum. And then there was the loud click of the phone being replaced on the hook. Ella hurried back to her bedroom and sat on her bed. Kelsi's footsteps sounded down the hall, and she appeared in the bedroom doorway. Her eyes were wide and bewildered. Her shoulders were stooped when she sat down on the bed.

"Kelsi?" Ella touched her arm. "Kels, what's wrong?"

Kelsi stared at her knees for a long time. She shook her head. "I broke up with Peter."

Ella's hand flew to her mouth. "Oh God." Her first impulse was to hug her sister. She wrapped her arms around Kelsi before she could even begin to process the information.

"He said if I wasn't ready to take the relationship to the next level, he wasn't interested." Kelsi pressed her left hand against her forehead. "Can you believe that? I mean, can you believe how cliché?"

Ella kept holding her sister tightly.

"He said he was tired of waiting." She stared at the mirror in front of them. "I told him he was an asshole."

Ella's heart was pounding while different thoughts vied for a position in her brain. Kelsi had actually called someone an asshole. Kelsi wasn't with Peter anymore. Kelsi and Peter hadn't had sex. Her mind flew to the French cancan ensemble Kelsi had bought. "But, I thought you were going to . . ."

Kelsi's shoulders heaved. "I thought I was, too, but then I changed my mind. I mean, I started to feel that that was all he wanted from me, and there's no way . . . That's not how I want it to be the first time." She fell back on the bed, her eyes went glassy, and tears started to dribble out and roll down the sides of her face. Ella had never seen her sister so ill-composed.

"Kels, I'm so sorry." She really, really was.

"It's okay." Kelsi pinched the area between her eyebrows with her thumb and forefinger. She sniffed. "I don't think I'm gonna go to the bonfire."

"Yeah, of course," Ella said, curling up next to her. "Do you want me to stay with you?"

"No," Kelsi whimpered. "I'd rather you go. Make an excuse for me. If he shows up . . ."

"He won't show up." He wouldn't, would he?

"But if he does, looking for me or something, just tell him I went away for the weekend. I don't care. I just don't want him to come here."

Ella nodded. She wanted to stay. She wanted to go. She wanted to see Peter so badly now, worse than she had before, and she hated that.

"I really just want to be alone," Kelsi said, sniffling. "I don't know why I'm crying. I guess I *wanted* him to be the one. But he's not right. He can't be the first one for me."

Ella looked around the room, searching for her favorite silky pillow. It was lying beside her bed. She picked it up and tucked it between Kelsi's arms.

Kelsi rested her cheek on it. "Thanks, El." She looked skinny and frail and beautiful. Ella turned off the light and turned on the fan so that Kelsi would be more comfortable.

In the hallway, Ella checked herself one last time in the mirror. On top of all the other emotions racing through her body — elation, sympathy, and nervousness — she felt something nagging and angry gnawing at her insides. It was half covered up by her wondering if she looked okay, in case Peter really did show. It wasn't something she wanted to think about.

But if she had stopped to dissect it, it wouldn't have taken long to figure out that — at least a little — she was hating herself.

"Where is everybody?"

Beth was the only one at the bonfire when Ella arrived. Ella looked at her watch. It was 9:43.

"Who knows?" Beth said. She sounded pissed. "You want a beer? Thanks for getting it, by the way." She popped open a blue cooler and held out a can of Bud Lite. Ella took it and sat on the sand. She looked both ways down the beach.

"Where's Kelsi?" Beth asked, drawing a frowning face in the damp sand with a stick.

Ella cast around for an excuse. She didn't know what Kelsi would want her to say. "She's not feeling well. Cramps."

"That sucks. But she'll be okay. It's not something a little Advil can't cure," Beth said, sounding annoyed.

Ella bit her lip. Beth had made her and Kelsi promise they were coming. Now even George, the birthday boy, wasn't here, and Beth's expression — in the flickering, meager light of the fire — was thunderous. The air was so thick with the moisture of impending rain that Ella's skin felt damp, reminding her she should have worn something warmer. Maybe the night was doomed in general.

"Well, here's somebody," Beth said, looking inland to where the houses met the beach. Ella turned and her heart caught in her throat. Peter was coming toward them with one hand in his shorts pocket, the other holding a cigarette. He was wearing a baseball cap, and as he walked, the breeze blew his loose navy blue T-shirt, exposing a tiny sliver of tan stomach. He tapped the cigarette as he arrived at the edge of the fire.

"Hey," he muttered, his eyes on Ella.

"Kelsi's not feeling well," Beth offered. "She's back at the house."

"Okay." Peter sat down next to Ella and without waiting for an offer, pulled the lid off the cooler and grabbed a beer. Beth stared at him, her head tilted quizzically.

Anybody else would have made small talk, or made some excuse about why he was here with people he didn't know when his girlfriend wasn't coming. But Peter just cracked open his beer and stared at Ella while Beth stared at him.

"Well, in case you're wondering where the rest of the crew is, Peter," Beth said dryly, breaking the silence, "George and Cara are probably fooling around somewhere. Jamie is most likely hiding in her bed."

"Oh, yeah?"

"We knew we could count on Ella here. She's always up for a good time," Beth said.

The way Peter smirked when Beth said this reminded Ella of every place where her skin met the silk of her lingerie. Peter stubbed out his cigarette and took a couple of long gulps of beer.

"Well, I'm gonna head down the beach," he said, standing up. "Thanks for the beer."

He gave a casual wave before sticking his free hand back in his pocket, and then he started walking. Ella's gut wrenched. Kelsi had gotten small in her mind over the past few minutes, and Peter had gotten big. Now it seemed like the line that always stood between Peter and her had vanished. She was free to do what she wanted.

Ella eyed Beth, who was staring off into space. It would be beyond suspicious if she followed him.

"That guy's weird," Beth said flippantly, flopping onto her back, her blonde hair spilling out behind her on the sand.

"I forgot something," Ella said, standing up abruptly.

"What?" Beth asked.

"Um, I have to go to the bathroom."

"You forgot you had to go to the bathroom?"

"Yep. I'll be back." She started backing away. She ignored the disappointment on Beth's face. There were much bigger things she could feel guilty about.

Ella headed up the beach toward the cottages, the opposite direction that Peter had gone, checking first to make sure his car was still in the parking lot. Once she reached the lot, she walked an extra block inland, then doubled back along a street that ran parallel to the ocean. Her breath was coming in short gasps, like when she used to play hide-and-seek as a kid. She didn't turn back toward the beach until she was sure she'd passed the bonfire. Then she headed down to the sand and pulled off her platform flip-flops. The light was dim, with the sky being so cloudy, but the street lamps helped illuminate the beach. For as far as she could see in either direction, it was empty. Had she gone too far?

She kept walking — away from the bonfire, toward where the houses completely fell off and it was just beach and dunes and rocky outcroppings into the water. She stopped and turned to look behind her. Maybe she'd overshot him. Maybe he'd gone back to his car and gone home. A lump formed in her throat.

She needed to see him tonight. She needed to know what

happened next. It hadn't been so urgent just half an hour ago, when he and Kelsi were still together, but it was urgent now.

Ella walked into the dunes, not knowing what else to do. She climbed the first mound of loose sand, her feet sinking with each step. She descended to a small valley, then climbed again. She reached the top and froze. Down the hill in front of her, Peter was lying on his back, his body propped up against the next rise. He'd taken his shirt off and tucked it behind his head. He looked incredible, sprawled against the sand, his bronze skin glinting in the moonlight. Ella looked at his flat stomach and noticed that the top button of his shorts was undone. She caught her breath. Ella wasn't sure he had seen her yet, though his body was directly facing her.

"Peter," she said tentatively. He lifted his head, then sat up. "I wanted to . . ." she began, but Peter raised a finger to his lips.

"No one is allowed to talk until they've taken their shirt off," he said. Ella smiled at the joke, but Peter didn't. Her feet felt sturdy in the sand now as she made her way toward him. Her pulse pounded in her ears. Suddenly, she didn't feel the cold at all.

She kept her eyes on his as she reached back, untied her halter top, and then pulled it off entirely.

21

Beth was lying on her back, checking out the stars. It wasn't hard, considering there were only about six or seven peeping through the clouds. The moist air made her skin clammy. She rubbed her upper arms, then put a hand to her throat. She thought she was going to cry.

"Look who we found down the beach."

Beth jerked up. George and Cara, with Jamie in tow, were approaching the edge of the fire. George had his arm wrapped around Jamie. "A lone mermaid washed ashore."

"Oh, God, I love *The Little Mermaid,*" Cara added. Beth didn't crack a smile.

George caught her eye, then widened his own eyes as he took in the deserted fire. He looked at his watch. "Are we late?"

Beth put her index fingers in the sand on either side of her waist and drew concentric circles. She didn't reply.

"Oh." George crouched and popped open the cooler. "We better start catching up then. Beer?" He offered a can to Cara, who took it, and then to Jamie, who shook her head. He popped open his own and took a few long gulps. "I have to say, Beth, I thought we'd get rained out. But you were right, as always." He sank down on the sand beside her. Beth just shrugged.

"I've never had a bonfire on the beach before," Cara chirped. "I mean, it's one of those things you always think you're going to do, but never get around to it. It's such a great idea, though." She looked out at the ocean, running a hand through her perfect hair, which was down and wavy tonight, silky as an actual mermaid's. "Isn't it cool down here in the dark?"

"Bonfires are the best," George said, sitting cross-legged. Beth could feel his eyes on her for a moment. She looked back at him, and he glanced away. George never managed to get a real tan like everyone else. In the dim moonlight, he glowed.

Cara seemed to notice it at the exact same time Beth did. She turned to him and gave him an exaggerated once-over. "Did somebody turn on a black light?"

"Ha, ha." George put his arm around her and pulled her onto the sand.

"Ha," Beth said sarcastically. Suddenly, Cara was even more perfect than ever.

George sat up again, polished off his beer, and opened another one. He dunked the base of the empty can into one of the sand mounds Beth had made earlier on, the metal and sand crunching together. His eyes met Beth's again, over the top of the can as he gulped. He tilted his head back and placed the can perpendicular to his mouth, his Adam's apple bobbing. He finished the beer in a matter of seconds and leaned into the cooler for another.

"You think maybe you should slow down, George?" Beth didn't bother to keep the sternness out of her voice. George hardly ever drank, because more than a can of beer could knock him flat.

George winked at her. "I don't think so, Mom." He popped the top loudly.

"Want me to go get the beer bong?"

George pulled the can away from his mouth, mid-sip, and said lazily, "Are you auditioning for Miss Bitch U.S.A.?"

Everyone sat in silence for a moment. Beth felt like she'd been punched in the stomach. "Whoa," Jamie breathed, finally.

"If all you ladies will excuse me." George stood abruptly and stripped off his shirt, then bent over to pick up his beer. "I'm getting naked. Who's coming with?"

Cara put her hand to her collarbone. "You mean, skinny-dipping?" Everyone looked at her. She laughed. "Wow." She stood with an air of determination. "Okay." As if everyone were pressuring her, or more likely, as if George had asked *her,* specifically.

"Beth?" George raised his eyebrows at her, a peace offering. He knew Beth was always up for skinny-dipping. Last summer they'd gone a couple of times with Ella and Kelsi. Cara stood beside him and brushed at some sand where it had gathered on his elbows.

"No, thanks." Beth avoided his eyes, and tried not to look at his chest. She ended up staring at some invisible point just beyond his head.

"Jamie?" George asked.

"I think I'm going to pass." Jamie wrapped her arms around her knees, as if somebody might actually force her to get naked. She looked petrified. "I'm not a skinny-dipper."

"Jamie!" George put his hand to his heart as if he'd been stabbed. "Not a skinny-dipper? Don't you know skinny-dipping is as close to heaven as a human being can get?"

Jamie shook her head. "No, I didn't know that, George."

"Well, now you do. C'mon."

"Please, George. I hate being naked."

George's eyes widened. "*Hate* being *naked*? How is that pos —"

"Jamie and I are gonna go for a walk," Beth said abruptly to the spot beyond George's head. She didn't think she could take watching George and Cara naked in the water together. She didn't think she could take seeing George naked at all. And anyway, Jamie obviously didn't want to go swimming. Sometimes George didn't know when to quit. He was clearly drunk.

She and Jamie watched as the pair headed toward the water, which because of low tide, was about a hundred yards away. Beth could see them peeling off their clothes and hobbling along, getting smaller. "Jackasses," Beth said as she scooted closer to Jamie.

"Does it make you jealous?" Jamie asked.

"What?"

"George and that girl."

"No. Who cares? He's so in over his head, it isn't even funny."

Silence.

"He's a guy. He thinks with his dick," Beth said nonchalantly. She felt as if saying things like this might actually become second nature to her if she kept it up for much longer.

"Do you really believe that about guys? That they only think with their penises?" Jamie asked earnestly.

Beth shrugged. Truly, maybe George didn't. Cara was annoying,

144

but maybe he didn't see her that way. She remembered the girl they'd seen at the minigolf course at the beginning of the summer. Maybe being girly was something you just had to do. Maybe it didn't make you any less of a person.

"Let's walk," she said to Jamie. They both rose and brushed the sand off their legs.

Beth's eyes lit on something on the ground. "Just a sec." She grabbed George's shirt from where he'd dropped it, then went running off in search of his shorts and boxers, kicking up sandy mud behind her as she got closer to the water. She could see him, splashing out there, surrounded by white foam waves. He and Cara were two separate figures, and then they merged for a second, and parted. Beth tried not to think about them kissing naked.

Standing there and looking at them in the water, Beth caught her breath sharply. She didn't want to see them together, but at the same time, she *needed* to watch. Suddenly, she realized that she might have been the one who was in way over her head. *I want to be where Cara is,* she thought, her cheeks flaming with desire and embarrassment. *It should be* me *who's out there alone with George.* She understood it now, the mix of all those strange emotions that had been tugging at her heart all summer long. It was quite simple, actually. She really *was* in love with George. There could be no more denying it. She turned away from the water, and spotted Cara's stuff in a neat, tiny pile not far from the water. Beth left it alone.

Back where the road bordered the sand, she dropped George's clothes underneath a streetlight, where a collection of A-frame houses with huge windows marked the beginning of town. She made sure the clothes were well into the circle of light, then

145

stepped over the curb. That way, he'd be naked on a floodlit stage. For only a minute, Beth wondered, *What am I doing?*

Jamie caught up and walked alongside her, but turned once to look back at the water.

"I'd be jealous," Jamie said, her curly hair rustling against her shoulders in the breeze. "George is supposed to be yours."

Twenty minutes later, Beth and Jamie were turning onto Conch Road, which ran straight through two neat rows of houses. They'd been silent for the past few minutes, spying through the windows of the houses whose lights were still on. They could see people watching TV, empty rooms filled with furniture, a middle-aged lady knitting. Jamie stuck her thumbnail in her mouth.

"Beth, I did something stupid."

"What?"

Jamie hesitated, her head tilted thoughtfully. Beth wondered what it was like to be that delicate. She almost felt jealous of Jamie, even when she was clearly so miserable. She was soft in all the places Beth was hard.

"I just really messed up. I broke something of Ethan's on purpose. I don't know how I'm going to fix it."

Beth stared at the street beneath their feet, deep in thought. "What was it?"

Jamie shook her head. "Just this thing he made. It doesn't really matter. It's just . . . I ruined it. I don't know what I was thinking."

Beth shrugged. "You were probably thinking you were pissed off."

"No. I'm not pissed off. I don't have anything to be pissed off about."

Beth stared hard at Jamie. "C'mon. Jamie, the guy dumped you."

"Yeah."

They both stopped to look in the triangular windows of a giant A-frame. A man and a woman were lying on the couch watching TV, fitted together like two spoons.

"But maybe I was too . . . I shouldn't have thought there was so much there. I just feel . . . so hugely stupid."

"Oh God, everybody's stupid," Beth gushed. "You need to find a guy who lets you know it's okay to be stupid." Of course, she was thinking about George. He always made her feel like her stupidities were cool.

Jamie thrust her hands into the pockets of her overalls, unconvinced.

Beth thought hard, trying to do better. She needed to separate herself from the George situation long enough to actually be helpful, but it was hard. She could only say what sounded right, hypothetically. "Look, maybe you're just trying too hard to hold on to something that you can't hold on to. Maybe there was never any way to keep that guy. If he let you go, he probably wasn't even worth keeping."

"Yeah."

Beth swallowed, feeling useless. Oh God. She loved George. She couldn't stop thinking about him. She missed him like crazy, even though they'd only been apart for these twenty minutes. Out of nowhere, tears pooled up in her eyes. Beth looked back over her shoulder toward the water. For all she knew, Cara and George were having sex on the beach with the waves crashing over them, like in that old movie *From Here to Eternity*. It was too much.

She and Jamie took a right onto Peachtree.

"I CAN'T SEE THEM ANYWHERE!"

The voice came from up the street ahead of them. Somebody was yelling at the top of their lungs, and of course Beth knew immediately who it was. She started hurrying toward the sound, Jamie trailing behind her. After a few seconds, she could just make out Cara up ahead. She was bent over laughing so hard she looked like she was going to pee her pants. Beth scanned the space around her for George. To the right, a light popped on, illuminating the windows of a low white ranch house.

"I think somebody HID THEM." *Crap.* Beth craned her neck upward, sucking in her breath. He wasn't . . .

George was on the roof of a green split-level on the left, his naked body lit against the dark sky. With his free hand, he was exaggeratedly scanning the horizon like a sailor. His other hand covered himself in front. "I wonder WHO did it? I wonder if it's because they're MAD AT ME."

Cara giggled and held her fingers over her lips to try to shush George, but it came out as part of the giggle.

"God." Beth walked up to the foot of the house. "George," she hissed. "Get down."

George threw his shoulders back and widened his eyes, as if he was surprised to see her. "Beth! Tell me, do you have any idea where my clothes might be?" Beth could hear the undercurrent of anger that ran behind the words. His face looked like the normal, goofy George. Only his eyes were angry.

"George, do you hear me? Get the hell down from there!"

Suddenly, a red-and-blue flash ran the length of George's body and the house, lighting up the trees. "Shit, cops," Cara said, and dashed off toward the woods. Jamie sprinted in the opposite direction, toward the beach.

Beth looked down the street, then back up at George. The flashing lights of the police car seemed to recede. "George, come on. It isn't funny. Get down."

"Not until you tell me what the hell your problem is."

"My problem is that you're on the roof. You're gonna fall."

"You better apologize," George said, now using both hands to cover himself down there. He swayed slightly on his feet.

"God, George. Please come down."

"Say you're sorry for acting like such a bitch."

"Whatever, I'm sorry. Come down."

George seemed to consider the situation for a second. Then he turned and padded toward the back of the house. Beth hurried around into the backyard, keeping her eyes on him for as long as she could. There was a lattice covered in roses that stretched from the ground to about two feet below the roof. George climbed down it gingerly while Beth averted her eyes. He fell the last couple of feet.

Beth crouched down beside him on the grass. "Are you okay?"

"Yeah."

He rolled over, wincing, seeming to forget he was naked. Beth tried not to let her eyes travel south, but she couldn't help it. They scanned downward and her skin started prickling. George tilted his chin against his chest and peered at her, which made her clear her throat and look at the grass. She'd seen him naked before. Just last summer, in fact. But she'd never really looked.

"C'mon, we gotta go," she hissed. She put a hand on his wrist, noticing the feel of the skin against her fingertips, and yanked him up. They ran toward the woods at the far end of the street. Once they reached the trees, they stopped and breathed hard for a second. Beth peered down the length of Peachtree, then up Oceanview Drive.

In another second, the police car appeared at the far end of the road. Beth tugged George back into the woods, her heart beating faster than it should have been. She was as excited as she'd ever been in her life. Silently, stealthily, they stole away — one girl in a too-big T-shirt and one skinny boy, naked and pale but undeniably cute, alone in the dark, hand in hand, running away to places unknown.

22

Ella stood in just her shorts and her strapless bra. She waited for Peter to do or say something, but he didn't move from where he sat. She tucked her thumbs into the waistband, her own fingers feeling strange against her skin, waiting some more.

Ella was trembling with anticipation. "Aren't you going to get up?"

Peter shook his head, just slightly, coolly. In the dimness, Ella could see his Adam's apple bob once. Her chest shuddered slightly as she breathed. She'd worn less than she was wearing now to plenty of family gatherings, but she'd never felt so naked. She couldn't bring herself to take the shorts off, too.

Where had this timid, unsure Ella come from? She didn't want her to stay. Boldly, suddenly resolved, she took the few steps between them and drifted down to her knees on the sand. She leaned over Peter and gently touched her mouth to his. She could feel his smile against her lips.

She pulled back, gazed into his dark eyes, and then leaned in to kiss him again. This time, neither one of them was gentle. Peter's tongue was in her mouth, and Ella sucked on it. She knew that trick could drive boys crazy. And Peter was no exception. He floated his hands to her thighs and stroked her skin. She could feel how much he wanted her.

Ella let out a sigh of pleasure. She felt her old confidence — which she'd lost somewhere at the beginning of the summer — flooding back. She stopped kissing Peter for a second and traced the curve of his strong jaw with one finger. "I have you," she whispered. Finally, she did.

He responded by trailing his finger along her cleavage. Then he buried his head in her neck, kissing her throat. "You do," he breathed against her ear. "You're amazing."

It was all Ella had needed to hear, all summer long. *Poor Kelsi, to miss this feeling,* Ella thought, as Peter dipped her back, his mouth still pressed against her neck. She wondered if her sister had ever had it, or would ever have it with anyone. Peter pressed her against the sand, and she rested her hand on the zipper of his shorts. He ducked his head and kissed his way down to her stomach.

"I am, huh?" she asked. He nodded, his lips grazing her belly button.

Arching her back, Ella guided his hands around to the clasp on her bra. As he unhooked it, she made sure to keep her eyes on his. She was controlling her own destiny. She was Supergirl.

"Prove it to me."

Of course, Peter didn't waste any time trying.

As he removed her bra, it started to rain. The freezing drops pattered down on Ella's breasts, but she didn't feel cold at all. Ella reached for Peter's zipper again and he eased her out of her tiny shorts. Before he took his own shorts off, Peter reached into his back pocket for something. Ella recognized the red, square foil packet. It was a condom. *This is it,* Ella thought, ecstatic and feverish and wanting him more than ever. For the briefest of moments, an image of Kelsi, alone at home, flashed through her mind.

But there was no turning back now.

23

Jamie stood above the remnants of the night's bonfire, kicking sand onto it to smother the flames. By now, the orange glow had been reduced to a flicker and a few tiny embers. It wasn't really much of a bonfire at all anymore. It was just a pile of logs. There was no use worrying about it, anyway, since it was going to pour soon.

She stopped kicking and crossed her arms over her chest, staring across the wide expanse of beach at the water. She wondered if Beth and George had made it home all right. She wondered why she'd come back to put the fire out in the first place.

The whites of the waves were clearly visible across the sand. Jamie kept her eyes trained on them, her mind drifting. She couldn't stop thinking. About what Beth had said. About the Millennium Falcon. About Ethan's poems. She took a few steps toward the water, her legs moving her forward as her thoughts tumbled out of control.

Beth had said that maybe Ethan hadn't been worth keeping. Jamie had heard the line before. But that was something she never really considered before. There'd never been any doubt in her mind that Ethan was the type of guy she wanted to be with. The only doubt that kept popping into her head was aimed solely at her own self.

"Wasn't I worth keeping?" she thought, gazing at the sleeping seagulls who had made their homes on the beach. She walked to the edge of the water and rubbed at the soreness that had been lingering in her throat all night long. She felt like she was going to have another breakdown.

But before that could happen, Jamie began to think about Ethan's poems and how she'd thought they were so much better than hers for quite some time. But now they just seemed stale and silly to her — like they belonged to someone imperfect, someone as imperfect as Jamie. She thought about the Millennium Falcon and how she'd admired all the work that had gone into it. But she hadn't ever really appreciated how much work she herself put into everything she did — her stupid dog hats, her silly sketches. She thought about trying to win Ethan back and how she'd screwed it up. Yet, right now, what she'd done seemed almost brave.

Nobody could say she hadn't tried her best. She'd tried her best at being a girlfriend. She *had* been worth keeping.

Jamie wanted to scream, she was so angry. She wanted to run somewhere, to hit something, to yell at someone. And what she really wanted, more than any of that, was to get in the water.

She peered both ways down the beach to make sure nobody was around. Slowly and nervously, Jamie unhooked both clasps of her overalls and let them drop to her feet. She looked around the beach again, and pulled her underwear down, too, and then tugged her shirt over her head and removed her bra. Covering her chest with her arms, she walked to the edge of the water and waded in.

She took a deep breath in preparation, even though the water wasn't really that cold. She just had to get used to the idea of swimming naked. Only when the water came up to her shoulders did she relax somewhat. After a few minutes of floating around, she finally felt comfortable. She began to do strokes — farther out, then back, keeping her head above the water.

The ocean cradled Jamie as if she were a child, and she felt beautiful and complete. Putting it off until the last moment, she finally submerged herself all at once. She had never felt this invigorated before.

A few seconds after she came up, it started to rain — first in slow, fat drops, then harder. The sudden shower pattered on her head and the water around her. It sounded like the crinkling of a plastic bag. Jamie let her body float up so that she was lying flat and exposed to the drops, her eyes closed. She drifted slowly away into the darkness.

George had been right. It *was* the closest thing to heaven.

24

Beth left George in the woods while she ran to get his clothes. They were still in the spot where she'd left them, in the circular glow of one of the streetlamps by the beach. She scooped them up quickly, peering around to make sure the cops hadn't come this way, and then scurried back toward the brush.

Still covering himself, George took them from her. Beth averted her eyes as he pulled on his boxers.

"Come on, Beth. I know you wanna look," he joked. "I'm irresistible." Beth met his eyes, trying to appear amused and instead feeling caught. Water was still dripping from his hair. He was smiling from ear to ear, which meant he could be very happy or very, very drunk.

"We should stay off the roads," Beth said. They could have gone to the right and gotten home along the deserted portion of beach, but it was shorter to just cut straight across the marsh. George took her wrist and pulled her along into the tall grass and mud. Somehow, Beth thought, holding on to each other like this felt so right.

The stars weren't so great here, surprisingly. Maybe it was because so many towns close together were giving off too much light. But from the marsh, it was hard to tell that there were any towns nearby at all. The reeds stood almost shoulder height and the way they blocked out all signs of civilization made Beth feel as if she were light-years away from home and anyone who thought they knew her.

"What time do you think it is?" she asked.

"Twelve-ish?"

Their feet made sucking sounds in the mud. *Sloosh, sloosh, sloosh, sloosh. George, Beth, George, Beth.* They were silent for a long time.

Ahead of them, a group of birds rose up. They seemed to go by in slow motion. Beth thought they were beautiful — just a bunch of bird-shaped shadows. She and George both paused to watch them.

"I knew I should have brought my shotgun," he said in a Southern accent, then burped.

"The comedy never stops," Beth said and began walking ahead. That is, until she suddenly felt all wobbly and let out a big yelp.

She tripped and instinctually grabbed onto George for support. He bobbled a bit, but managed to stay rooted, and when she'd finally gotten her balance, they both looked down at her right foot where her sneaker had once been. Now, it was conspicuously bare. Somehow, the sneaker had gotten stuck in the thick mud.

"I guess I should have tied my laces tighter," Beth said with a snicker. She poked around in the mud a bit. But there was a whole lot of nothing down there.

"Forget it, I'll just hop the rest of the way," Beth said with a shrug. "Remember how we won that three-legged race last year at the Memorial Day picnic? I've still got the skills."

"I'm sure you do, champ," George said as he let her lean her left arm on his shoulder and she started jumping forward with her one bare foot up in the air. *Sloosh, sloosh, slurk.*

"Yeah, this isn't working. You're totally slowing us down, gimpy. Why don't I just give you a piggyback?" George suggested. He bent down to give her a boost.

"Nah, that's quite all right." Wrapping her thighs around George's body would just be too weird right now.

"C'mon, Bethy. I can handle it. You always think I'm a wimp."

"Because you are a wimp," she joked, but he didn't laugh.

Suddenly, it was a weird moment. George was breathing close to her and he looked very serious. He was probably still mad about the whole clothes-napping incident. Of course, he had every right to be.

"Okay," she said, turning him around so that his back faced her. She put her hands on his shoulders and let him know she was on the way up. "You're not a wimp."

He crouched as she hopped onto his back, her legs squeezing around his waist. She was keenly aware she was breathing on his neck.

With George's feet sinking deeper in the mud, they started the trek home.

*　　*　　*

"Hold on tighter."

"If you had a butt, I wouldn't be sliding off."

"You're supposed to be an athlete. Use those thigh muscles and hang in there."

Writhing with embarrassment, Beth let go of George's neck and slid to the ground, holding her bare foot up gingerly.

"Well, I need something to work with. You know, like meat on your bones?"

George was breathing heavily from the exertion. "What you need is a freight train."

"Asshole," she said under her breath, orienting herself. "Hey, where the hell are we?"

"The road's just up there. See it?"

George pointed to a clearing up ahead, but it felt wrong to Beth. It didn't seem that the road to home should be there. But it was too dark to see clearly.

Beth started walking, not worrying about her bare foot anymore or what might be under the mud.

George caught up with her, and they both reached the clearing at the same time.

"George!"

The "road" was actually the beach. They could see the string of cottages, but they were across the inlet.

"George! How did you get us across the water from where we're supposed to be? I mean, how is that possible?"

George just shrugged. He didn't look worried. Beth wasn't worried either, really — they weren't that far away. They must have veered too far east. At low tide, they could have waded across. But now . . .

"We're gonna have to swim for it," George said.

"Swim?"

"Yeah — otherwise we have to walk around that way." He gestured back toward the way they'd come. "It'll take forever."

"Fine. But don't think that I'm going to get naked."

George covered his now-clothed lower half with one hand and his chest with another, making a horrified face. "Are you suggesting *I* want to?"

They waded in slowly, hoping that they wouldn't step in some hole that they couldn't see. Then they'd be drenched from head to toe.

"I feel like a castaway," Beth said. She still didn't want to let on how much she was loving being out here with him, alone like this.

"I wonder what kind of critters are in here at night," George mused.

Beth smacked him playfully. "That's a wonderful thought. Thanks for sharing."

They were up to their waists now.

"Jellyfish? Horseshoe crabs? Water snakes?"

"George, could you knock it off?"

"Okay, okay. Didn't know you were such a wuss."

The water began to part in ripples around them. Somewhere, a heron croaked and flapped, which startled both of them.

They crested the opposite shore within minutes, wet up to their shoulders. Beth's waterlogged denim shorts dragged as she waded out onto the beach and sank onto the sand. George came out pretending to be a paratrooper, using his elbows and knees to drag himself up.

"That's a great lobster impersonation, George. Bravo," Beth said and applauded mockingly.

He came to his knees, raising his arms above his head like a wrestler, and then flopped onto the beach next to her. He rolled onto his back, breathing hard, the back of his head sinking into the sand. Beth did the same.

How many nights had they spent like this — staying out late, lying around, alone together with nothing else to do? Only tonight Beth felt that the tension between them was as tangible as a third person. It took the shape of Cara, splayed out there on the sand seductively, her perfect mermaid hair fanning out in all directions.

Beth felt now was as good a time as any to let her guard down. "I'm sorry, George. About what I said today."

George was silent for a second. "It's okay." He looked over at her, narrowing his eyes. "You don't like Cara, do you?"

Beth shrugged. "I don't know her."

"You think she's lame, right?"

Beth shrugged. "George, like I said, I don't know her enough to judge either way."

"Maybe she's, you know, too girly for you," George said matter-of-factly and without the slightest hint of sarcasm. He didn't mean it to hurt. He was just good ol' drunk and honest.

"God," Beth sat up in frustration and wrapped her arms around her knees.

George peered up at her, his arms beneath his head. "What's the matter?"

She let out a breath, half laughing. "Nothing."

She felt his hand reach out and touch her shoulder. "Seriously, Beth. Why are you mad at me?"

162

"*I'm* a girl," Beth said.

This got his attention. He sat up now. "I know that. I didn't mean it to come out like that." He had a straightforward way of looking at her that made her feel guilty. She wasn't being truthful with him, and it was getting harder and harder to keep her mouth shut.

"I feel kind of like you're going to forget about me," she finally whispered.

George tilted his head to the side. Beth couldn't tell if he was wincing or concentrating. His eyes had gotten wide under his long lashes. Then the look simply disappeared, and the wall between them dropped. Suddenly, George assumed his usual goofy expression.

He squinted and then whispered, "Are you jealous?"

Beth shook her head, half laughing again. "No." Thank God it was dark. Thank God, thank God, thank God. Her face was on fire.

"Beth."

She shook her head, rolling her eyes.

"I think you are," he said.

Beth slapped him on the arm. "No, I'm not. Shut up."

"Oh?" He flipped over onto all fours, at her side. It was a game now to him. "Beth's jealous? *Rrrrrrrrr.*" He grabbed her hard around the shoulders and rubbed the top of her head. He hugged her so hard that she went down again onto her back.

"You are so cute," he said, looking down at her affectionately. "I could never forget about you, Bethy."

"Oh God." She clamped her hand over her eyes, secretly relieved. "You try to have a serious talk with someone . . ."

She felt her hands being tugged away from her face. "No really, I'm touched. Maybe we should have a special handshake, so you know I'll never abandon you." He took her hand and rubbed the palm. Beth sat up and yanked it away.

"I really care about you," George said. "Do you know that?"

"Please . . ." She started to stand up, annoyed at the thrill that rose in her chest when she heard him compliment her, even in his own stupid, joking way. She was just brushing the sand off her legs when he pulled her back down by her hand, and made a line across her palm with his nail.

"We can cut ourselves right here. No backing out this time, okay?" Beth loved the way he traced the line in her hand.

"You really should have slowed down on the Bud," she said. But still, she didn't move.

"Maybe." He looked at her steadily now.

"Well, we should . . ." She looked over her shoulder toward home.

"Beth." He had the wide-eyed look again, unguarded. He still had his fingers wrapped in hers. He breathed in loud, once. "Beth. Look at me. Don't be jealous."

Beth was like a person staring at a car accident. She couldn't look away.

He moved toward her and put his lips on hers, lightly. He moved his hands behind her head and held her there. Beth stayed perfectly still. She was convinced that if she moved, everything would disappear. She surrendered herself to the moment and opened her mouth to accept his kiss. She felt his tongue push against hers. Was this really happening?

It was crazy and surreal and absolutely wonderful. He tasted faintly like beer, but Beth felt like she couldn't get enough of him. She wanted to kiss him like this forever. George's fingers were tangled in her hair but then he moved his hands so he could cup her face, gently. He pulled back for a brief instant and studied her intently, as if he wanted to memorize her.

"Beth," he whispered. She could see her reflection in his eyes.

"George," she whispered back. It was the only thing, really, that she could say. It was like they were seeing each other for the first time.

Then they didn't need words anymore. He kissed her again, deeply, and he shifted so that she was on her back, and he was covering her. As Beth reached up to touch the back of his neck, her hand got jammed in his armpit, and for an instant she expected him to start laughing, as if the whole thing had been a joke. But George only brushed her hand away, and began sliding his own hands along her arms, then down to her stomach and hips and along her thighs, his mouth on hers the whole time. She pressed up against him to let him know she liked what he was doing. His breaths came quick now. He rolled her T-shirt up over her belly, and then Beth felt his hands on her breasts. *This is George,* she thought.

Suddenly, her skin felt like it was being tickled with a million feathers. And then she realized she *was* being tickled with rain.

George shoved himself back at the same time she noticed it. His face was flushed and his hair was pushed back at a messy angle. His eyes were beautiful. He and Beth stared at each other, still breathing hard. He looked up at the sky and gazed at it for a moment, like it was the first time in his life he'd seen rain. Then he focused back on Beth.

"Wow, sorry," he said, catching his breath.

Beth shook her head. "It's okay." She cleared her throat and smoothed back her hair. "You've had a lot to drink." She tried to think of some kind of joke to lighten things up, but none would come.

She rubbed at her lips, remembering the feel of his, and they both rose from the ground. Beth could feel blood rushing through her ears, her eyelids, and her fingers. She had been waiting for this for so long, and now it had happened. It was over so soon.

"You're probably tired," he said, peering out at the water beyond her shoulder. Raindrops were cascading down both of their faces.

"I think I'm gonna jump in the ocean again," George said after a moment. He started for the water, then glanced back briefly at Beth.

"Um, I should really get back," she said.

Beth felt like she had been conducting so much electricity that it was dangerous to get wet. Maybe electrocution wouldn't be such a bad thing. It couldn't hurt worse than what she was experiencing now.

"I'll catch up with you later, okay?" George said. "Get home safe."

He turned and walked to the shore, his head down.

Beth's mind was a blank. Her body felt so sensitive, it was almost sore.

She could have drawn a map of every place George had touched.

25

Ella dragged to a stop when she approached Peter's car, her fingers linked through his. The wet walk back from the beach had taken just a few minutes, but it felt like they had just finished a marathon. A lot had changed back on the dunes. She pulled off his baseball cap, which she'd snatched along the way, and handed it to him. "So, I guess I should probably walk home."

She half expected Peter to protest. Fat, juicy raindrops were still showering them. The air was biting at Ella's sensitive skin.

"Cool," Peter said. He pulled her close so that she was sandwiching him against his car.

"I had a good time," Ella said lamely. She wanted to kick herself for saying something like that because it felt flip. If anything, what just happened with Peter was one of the most incredible moments of her life. She'd had sex before. But never with a guy like that. And never in the pouring rain. "Well," she said, "do you want to hang out tomorrow?"

"I don't know. I've got some stuff to do. But I'll call you."

Peter's hair was plastered against the edges of his face in little wet triangles. He wrapped one arm around her neck and pulled her tight to his lips as they kissed, then pulled back and let go.

Ella tried to quell the rising panic in her belly. "Maybe you shouldn't call me, because of Kelsi." She put her fingertips on the waist of his shorts. "Maybe I should just call you." Ella thought about Kelsi at home, curled up in bed. Maybe they should talk about *that*.

"Cool." Shrugging, and then pulling his door open, Peter moved her backward with his right hand, then ducked inside the car.

Ella searched her head for the perfect thing to say, something that Peter would really remember her by. She kept hold of the door handle, staring at him. Maybe she was waiting to feel different. You were supposed to, right?

"I'll see you later." Peter pulled on the door from the inside, yanking the handle out of her grasp. He flashed her his gorgeous smile through the rain-streaked window, and then the car lurched into motion.

Ella stood still long enough to watch it disappear around the corner. She absentmindedly shoved her bangs back so that they were glued on either side of her forehead, away from her eyes. Then her mind started to trouble her.

Kelsi.

Ella couldn't help but feel like she'd just robbed her sister of something really wonderful. But at the same time, she also felt like she'd lost something very important. Her body felt empty and yet full all at once. It was like nothing she ever experienced before.

She pointed her feet in the direction of home and started

walking. She passed the backside of the Pebble Beach clubhouse, right by the pool enclosure. She'd learned to dive at that pool. The feeling she remembered from that day suddenly was far more exhilarating than what she felt now. Now, she felt more like . . . what was it? Words couldn't really describe the mix of emotions. But for some reason, the image of emptying an ashtray kept coming to mind. What was that supposed to mean?

Ella turned up on Oceanview Drive. She wished she'd asked Peter for a ride after all, at least to the edge of the dirt road. She had a severe case of the chills. The lights of the houses farther inland were all surrounded by hazy, foggy glows — making deceptively warm-looking halos around themselves. Ella crossed her arms tighter across her chest as she walked. She couldn't wait to get under her covers. She'd pull them over her head and try not to face Kelsi in the morning. She didn't know if she could.

She took a right onto the dirt road. All of the cottages were already dark. What time was it? Eleven? Twelve?

On the front stoop, she stepped out of her flip-flops and rubbed her feet on the wiry mat, then turned the knob. It didn't give. She tried it again to confirm that it was locked. Ella then headed around to the back deck.

She felt a slight tinge of annoyance with her dad for locking the door. What was he worried about, anyway — that they were going to get robbed by seagulls? She reached the stairs of the deck and began to tiptoe. She didn't think she was that late, but she slowed her breathing so she could make her entrance as silently as possible. She reached for the handle of the sliding glass door, her lips tightly closed, and listened to the stillness of the house.

"El."

Ella thought she'd imagined it at first, until her eyes caught the movement of a shape over at the deck table, under the giant green umbrella.

"Kelsi?"

At first it looked as if Kelsi was still in her pajamas, but as Ella got closer, she realized it was a white pullover and sweatpants. The clothes looked damp. A ball of fire lodged itself in Ella's throat. She stopped getting closer and prepared herself for the worst.

"Can you sit with me for a second?" Kelsi asked quietly.

Ella glanced at the door to the house. Once inside, she could hole up in the bathroom and take a bath.

"Ella, please."

Obediently, Ella ducked under the umbrella and sank against the plastic seat. The rain hitting the vinyl made a shrill sound that was almost deafening. Kelsi clasped her hands on the table and inclined her head, almost like she was listening for some melody in the rhythm of the drops.

"Why are you all wet?" It was all that Ella could bring herself to say.

"I decided to go to the bonfire." Kelsi paused and Ella's body began to go numb. Her legs felt like they were floating away. *Come back, you cowards!* she thought. She might need them to sprint at a moment's notice. "I didn't want to miss it just because . . ."

When she lifted her eyes to Ella, it was clear that she'd been crying. Hot knives seemed to stab Ella's skin. Did she know? If she did, how could Ella ever ask for forgiveness? Ella looked down at her hands so that she didn't have to make eye contact with Kelsi.

"I went down there and, you know, I drove because it looked like it was going to rain. And Peter's car was in the parking lot. Did he come to the bonfire?"

Ella decided to say no. But then, Beth had seen him. And Ella had a long history of lying: to her dad about dates back when she wasn't allowed to go on them, to her teachers about homework. She knew the best lies were the ones that were as close to the truth as possible. "Yeah," she admitted. "He came and had a beer and walked off."

"Really?" Kelsi said. "Because he wasn't around when I got there. Everybody was gone. Where'd you all run off to?" Kelsi looked at Ella intently as she waited for the answer.

Ella fidgeted. "Um, I had to go to the bathroom so I left. I don't know what happened with everyone else."

Kelsi took a long breath. Ella waited, paralyzed at the thought of her sister finding out what she had done.

"Well, I got back in my car and waited in the parking lot, just to see him come back, but he didn't for the longest time." Kelsi said, swallowing hard.

Ella nodded as if she had lost her voice.

"And then there he was." Kelsi rubbed one hand hard against her right cheek. Ella felt like she was going to pass out. "He and this girl, walking back up the beach. They were holding hands and everything. It was dark and rainy and they were really far away, but I know it was him. He was wearing this T-shirt I bought him at Abercrombie. I should have known. He's such a jerk."

Ella's hand, the one that had been holding Peter's earlier, snaked out and covered Kelsi's clasped fingers. She desperately wanted to hold on to her sister and make everything okay. Her heart was beating so hard, it could possibly crack a rib. Kelsi pulled her hand away and shook her head.

"I knew it, anyway." She rolled her eyes. "He was probably cheating on me the whole time. But you know what? It wasn't even worth confronting him. I just peeled out of there."

"Oh, Kelsi." Ella's arms felt too trembly and weak to wrap around Kelsi, despite the genuine pity she felt for her sister.

"You always thought he was an asshole, didn't you?" Kelsi asked, sniffling a little.

Ella nodded automatically, agreeing by default.

"I could tell you did."

They sat in silence for a few minutes.

Then Ella started to get antsy. She didn't dare ask, but she had to know exactly what her sister had seen. "Did you, um . . ." She cleared her throat. "What about the girl?"

Kelsi looked at her long and hard, then shrugged. "Who knows? Some random girl. One of many, I guess."

Ella finally found the strength to reach around her sister and pull her into a hug. She tried to think about what Kelsi might need to hear and mentally put herself in her sister's shoes.

"Don't feel bad, Kelsi. I mean, none of this is about you. Don't let him make you feel bad about yourself." That was how Ella would feel if some guy cheated on her. She'd feel like she wasn't as irresistible as she'd thought, and that would make her crazy.

Kelsi swiped at her eyes and blinked at Ella.

"I know. I don't feel bad about *myself*. I just feel bad that it didn't work out." She rubbed at her face with both hands now. "I was silly to think it might have been something more. I wonder if he loves that other girl."

Ella wondered, too. She wondered if she and Peter loved *each other*.

She didn't know. Was love supposed to feel like emptying an ashtray?

For a long time after they were in bed and the lights were out, Ella could hear that Kelsi was still awake. She tried to make her own breathing even, so that she could relax and finally get some sleep. It was hard, though, because of the feelings swirling around inside her. She didn't feel pretty or sexy or confident or triumphant. In fact, she felt hollow, as if someone had carved her like a pumpkin.

"El?" Kelsi's voice was low and unsure.

Ella thought about not answering. "Yeah."

"Where were you? I mean, you said went to the bathroom, but you weren't here when I got home."

"Oh," Ella croaked. She suddenly felt incredibly queasy. She cast about frantically for a story. "I went back to the bonfire afterward. But everyone was gone. So I . . . went for a walk."

"A walk?"

"Yeah."

"You hate walking."

"I like the rain."

"Oh." Kelsi was silent for a long time. "I never knew that about you."

Ella didn't reply. She waited for Kelsi to say more. But thankfully Kelsi's breathing tapered off into a slow, steady rhythm.

There were a lot of things Kelsi didn't know about her, Ella thought. And apparently, there were a lot of things Ella didn't know about anything.

For instance, she'd always thought that only boys could break your heart. But now she wondered if maybe sisters could, too. Ella felt as if hers might be in a million pieces, scattered all over the dunes.

Dear Ethan,

   I don't know if I'll ever send this letter, but I feel like I need to write it. The truth is, I have a lot to say to you.

   Jamie stuck her pen in her mouth and stared at the paper. She was sitting on the hammock in the backyard. The sea was indigo today, and everything around the peninsula felt soggy. It had rained most of the night. *I have a lot to say* was an easy place to start. But now it got sticky. How did she get everything she was feeling into word form? She needed to explain to Ethan that she didn't need him anymore. That she was getting over him. She wanted him to know that she was herself again, that she wasn't the pathetic girl she'd been all summer who'd tried to win him back.

We had some good times.

No, that was stupid and cliché. She crossed it out.

I thought that we meant something to each other.

That was better. It was honest.

I admit, you definitely meant something to me. I guess I'll always care about you in a certain way. But I want you to know that's not the way it is anymore.

Jamie's eyes started to blur. She kept writing as the tears forged a slow path down her cheeks.

I don't know what I really want from writing this letter. Mostly, what I'd like to do is take back some apologies, a lot of apologies I didn't even say but felt. I'm not sorry I hooked up with your friend. I'm not sorry for <u>not</u> wanting to be just friends with you. I'm not sorry for missing you, or for thinking we were more than we were. I'm not sorry for acting like somebody else to try to win you back.

I guess I'm not even sorry we had sex, though I guess part of me wishes I'd waited for someone else for my first time.

She could feel her face warming.

But you know, so what? In the future, I plan to be with someone who knows what I'm worth, and who's a million times better than you. Then what we had and did will just be part of my life's story. Trust me, it won't be the biggest part. Not even close.

There were tears on Jamie's lips when she smiled.

Ethan, I hope you have a nice life. I hope that if I run into you again someday, you will look terrible and I will look amazing. I hope you eat your heart out when it happens. But really, I don't care either way.

Jamie

A giggly feeling rose up in Jamie's chest as she read over the letter for a second and third time. It was good. Short, but sweet. Still, it was the kind of thing she could never in a million years bring herself to mail. But that didn't matter. Writing it was enough of a release, and that was why Jamie loved to write. It always helped her get to the root of her emotions.

At the end of the third read, she added a PS.

By the way, your poems suck.

After reading it for a fourth time, Jamie decided that it was too good to waste. She blew her nose with a tissue and called to her aunt.

"Aunt Claire, I have a letter to mail. Do you have any stamps?"

Aunt Claire was sitting on a recliner on the deck with Jordan in her lap. She was reading him a classic Curious George book. "I don't know," she said, as she stood up and led Jamie inside to where her purse was lying on the wooden chest by the door.

"Let's see. . . ." Aunt Claire pulled out her wallet and stuck her finger in the change pocket, then pulled out a tiny square of wax paper. "One twenty-cent stamp for postcards," she said apologetically. "Why don't you try next door?"

Jamie shrugged. "Nah. I feel like going for a bike ride, anyway. I'll just go into town."

She picked up her vintage beach bag and tucked the letter inside, then slung it over her shoulder and headed out the door. The Lemonde was parked against the shed.

Riding over the bumpy dirt road and then out onto the smooth pavement, Jamie felt the wind in her hair and remembered biking with Ethan. She'd been so joyful then. And although she wasn't feeling too joyful right now, she realized that, regardless of what happened, she was going to be okay. Sure, she wasn't dizzyingly happy. But okay was good enough for the moment, and eventually, she'd find that happiness in her heart again. It was just going to take some time.

The pavement had dark black patches from being soaked with rain. All around, the houses were dripping from last night's storm. Jamie thought she should write a poem about it. She started thinking of the verses in her head so she could jot them down when she got home.

Jamie was just reaching for the gleaming glass door of the Pebble Beach post office when she spied someone inside who was about to walk out. *Crap.*

She yanked her hand back and looked around for a place to hide. God, it would be humiliating to see him. She hurried down to the corner of the building and ducked into the parking lot, leaning her back against the wall. It was ridiculous, she knew. But there was no way she was moving. She waited at least a minute, then crept to the very edge of the wall and peered around.

"Am I not supposed to see you?"

Scott was standing there, wearing another trademark Hawaiian shirt — this one was yellow with crocodiles scattered all over it. It was so bright, it almost hurt to look directly at it.

Jamie managed to flash him a humble grin. "No, you're not." She cleared her throat. "Can you just pretend like you didn't?" She wanted to be a piece of gum melting into the sidewalk and then latching onto the bottom of someone's sneaker.

An amused smile crept onto Scott's face. "No, I don't think that's something I can do."

Jamie sighed and pulled away from the wall. She kicked her shoe into the pavement. "Look, I'm really sorry about everything. Especially the hitting part."

Scott laughed. "Every girl slaps some guy at some point, right? It's like a rite of passage."

Jamie tried to smile but only grimaced. "That's very nice of you to say. But there was no excuse for what I did. I'm really, really sorry."

Scott waved his hand dismissively. "Don't mention it, really. I was kind of drunk myself."

They both stood there silently for a second.

"Well . . ." Jamie started moving in a see-you-later gesture.

"What are you doing down here at the post office?"

Jamie bit her lip. "Mailing a letter . . . um, to Ethan." She couldn't believe she had just confided that much to Scott. Was she out of her mind?

"Whoa. That's awesome. What'd you say? Did you tell him to take a long walk off a short pier or something like that?"

She couldn't tell him. At least, that was Jamie's immediate impulse. And then she loosened up a bit. She didn't know Scott very well, but she did get the feeling that he was an easygoing person who you could tell just about anything to, and nothing would shock him. "I just kind of told him some immature stuff about how he sucks. It was something I felt like I needed to do."

Scott nodded solemnly.

"I hope, I mean, is it bad that I told you?"

Scott grinned. "You know, Ethan's my friend. But his ego's huge. He needs to be knocked off his pedestal every once in a while. And from what I've seen of your combat skills, you're just the girl to do it."

For the first time in a long while, Jamie let out a roar of a laugh. Scott had totally caught her off guard with his humor. It was great to feel so comfortable with someone again.

"So may I ask what *you're* doing here?" she asked, after regaining her composure.

"Just doing errands before work. Nothing special."

Jamie nodded. She knew he'd told her what kind of work he did, but she'd forgotten yet again. "Well, it was good seeing you," she said, moving to brush past him and head inside.

"Hey, wait a second." He put his hand on her arm lightly and hesitated for a moment. "After you mail that letter, wanna hang out for a while? I've got some interesting stuff lined up for this afternoon."

This time, Jamie was the one with the open, easy smile. Suddenly, there was nothing she felt like doing more.

27

A tattered *Marie Claire* lay on the bathroom counter. It had wet circular marks where Beth's fingers had touched it. She leaned over it now, making sure she had the quantities right.

Two eggs.

She cracked one and held it over the mixing bowl, waiting for the clear goop to separate itself from the shell. She did the same with the other egg.

One cup oatmeal.

One teaspoon milk.

Beth added the ingredients and then set the containers aside. She stuck a silver spoon into the bowl and stirred.

"Beth, don't you want to come to dinner?" her mom called from the other room.

"You go ahead, Mom. I'll be there in a few minutes."

Her mother's footsteps sounded down the hall and Beth looked at herself in the mirror. She tried to tell herself she wasn't doing this for George. But she knew that wasn't true.

She'd been hiding from George all day. She'd stayed in bed that morning until she was sure she'd heard him go out, then she'd gone for a long run around town. She'd come home hoping he wasn't there, and then she'd been disappointed when he wasn't. Then, since the waiting had been killing her, she'd borrowed one of Ella's magazines and started her little beauty ritual. And here she was. They'd definitely see each other at dinner. The thought made her feel ill.

She slathered the mixture onto her face.

Beth had never had a pedicure. She'd never used any body or hand lotion except Jergens Unscented. She never spent more than three minutes on her hair. It wasn't that she didn't like to do these things, it was just that she'd never seen herself as *that girl*.

Now she took her mom's Bath & Body Works Moonlight Path cream and rubbed it onto her freshly shaven legs. She tucked her hair back behind her ears.

While she waited for the mask to dry, she grabbed a lemon, sliced it in half like the picture on page eighty-nine showed, and rubbed it along her arms, concentrating on the elbows. *Marie Claire* seemed to hold the opinion that guys definitely notice if your elbows are soft or not.

But the question of the day was: Would George notice? George had kissed her. She and George had hooked up. But what did that mean? Would he dump Cara? Had it happened already? He was probably already at dinner, probably as nervous about facing Beth as she was about facing him. They'd have to talk about what had happened before he left tomorrow. But it was the last thing Beth wanted to do, especially if the discussion ended with it being hard for them to still be friends. That was the one thing she knew she couldn't handle.

She sat down on the closed seat of the toilet. The mask was starting to pinch at her pores. She wished last night hadn't ended like it did — so abruptly, and with George walking away. She needed to know if it had just been some drunken hookup, or if it was something more.

After a few minutes, Beth stood up and turned on the tap. She wet a washcloth and rubbed at her face in a "gentle, circular motion," just like the article instructed. Then she cupped more water in her palms and splashed off any remnants of egg. She dried her face and looked in the mirror, ready to see a new, more feminine, more — might as well just admit it — *Cara-like* Beth.

In the mirror, Beth's eyebrows were still straight, and not arched like Cara's. Her face looked plain to her.

Her heart sank. She should have figured. Nowhere in the recipe had *Marie Claire* promised a miracle.

"Beth." Ella's dad was standing over the grill. "I've never seen you late to a meal before."

"Ha, ha. You're such a comedian," Beth said, grabbing a plate from the table and holding it out for two hot dogs. She was in no mood for her uncle's teasing. She had already spied George at the second table, sandwiched between Kelsi and Ella. At least he wasn't sitting next to Cara, which was a good sign. But Cara *was* here. Again.

Beth debated whether or not to go sit with them but, at the last minute, wimped out and walked over to the circular kids' table where Jessi sat alone. She and George couldn't exactly talk with all the cousins around, anyway. Maybe he'd come over to her later, and they could finally get things out in the open.

"Why aren't you playing boccie ball?" Beth asked Jessi, nodding toward where Drew and Jordan were already deep into a game on the lawn.

Jessi sighed. "Everybody always fights."

Beth understood that feeling. It was true. Boccie ball could be extremely controversial.

"You're a wise girl, Jessi," she said appreciatively. She couldn't stop feeling as if George's eyes were on her back.

Jessi seemed pleased with her cousin's compliment and patted her leg. "You're pretty, Beth," she said.

"That was sweet. Thanks," Beth replied. Was it completely pathetic that she was truly flattered by Jessi's comment? Maybe it was her new beauty regimen. She was tempted to ask Jessi what, exactly, was pretty about her. Was it her skin? Her hair? But she couldn't stoop to that level. She was just biting into her hot dog when Ella walked past their table, looking a bit moodier than usual.

"But Ella's *really* pretty," Jessi added.

Beth ate in silence. She tried not to home in on George's voice a few feet away, but she couldn't help it. He was telling some story that she'd already heard, in his typical I-can't-hear-myself-unless-I-shout voice. Cara was laughing, and the butterflies in Beth's stomach flapped harder, frantic — as if someone had put them in a jar. Did the girl ever stop laughing at George's jokes? Didn't it get old?

Beth wondered if she should ask Jessi her opinion on a Beth/ Cara looks comparison. But then, she probably didn't want to know. Kids could be way too honest, sometimes. What Beth was just hoping for, though, was that George would walk up behind her any minute now. They were best friends — Cara or no Cara. If something was weird between them, they'd set it right.

When she finished her hot dogs, Beth did her best to stay seated, act casual, and wait patiently. But after half an hour, there was no tap on the shoulder, no George sitting down beside her on the bench. This was getting annoying.

Fine. She'd make the first move. She was brave enough. She'd ask him if they could walk somewhere and talk about . . . everything.

She stood up and turned around with the empty plate in her hand, her heart thudding.

George's table was empty.

"They walked down to the beach, sweetie," Aunt Claire said, picking up on Beth's look of total surprise. "Something about catching the sunset. You should go."

Beth looked at her watch. The sunset wasn't for another two hours. It was George's last night. He was driving home at dawn.

He hadn't even bothered to invite her.

28

"Are you all set back there?"

"What?"

"Are you ready?"

"What?"

Scott swiveled around until his face appeared over the back of his seat so that Jamie could see him. He looked both mirthful and concerned at the same time.

"I said, are you ready for me to go?"

Jamie nodded after reading his lips. Above the roar of the plane's engine, it was hard to hear herself think, much less hear Scott yelling from the front seat. She stared at the back of his head as he turned to face the control panel, wishing it were quieter so that she could ask him more questions. Like, what exactly made it possible for a tiny pile of metal like this to fly through the air. And whether he could promise her they wouldn't crash.

Instead, she tried some yoga breathing while she stared out the miniscule window to her left. It was a tiny runway, and Jamie could see Scott's dad standing in the archway of the hangar, grinning and waving at them. The few times Jamie had flown out to Arizona to visit her grandfather, taking off had seemed kind of mystical. At big airports, you felt like you were part of this huge machine that wouldn't — couldn't — let you fall.

The size of this airport, the fact that she had met the guy in the hangar waving at them, the fact that she knew the guy who'd be flying the plane — that he wore Hawaiian shirts and that they'd kissed — took away all the mystery of this flight. Jamie dug her nails into her knees and meditated some more.

The plane lurched into motion. Jamie's stomach lurched along with it. The grass lining the runway slid past them, slowly at first, and then faster and faster. Jamie tugged at her locket. And then the plane tilted up in front, and suddenly they were moving upward. She didn't know that they'd left the ground until she peered over her side of the plane and glanced down below them.

Ugh. It was dizzying. Jamie decided not to look outside anymore. Like all experiences, she needed to focus, to catalog this mentally for her writing. She homed in on the layout of the cockpit, the shrinking feeling in her stomach, and the sound of the engine, which, to her, seemed like it was struggling.

"The engine is making weird noises," she shouted at the back of Scott's head. He didn't turn around or budge.

"Scott?"

Nothing. They were still climbing, but not fast enough for Jamie to get that feeling of being pushed backward, like on larger planes. She leaned forward and tapped Scott on the head.

He didn't look back, but he gave her the thumbs-up and Jamie tried to calm down. She was definitely worrying too much. She gave him the thumbs-up, too, though he couldn't see it. Then she sank back into her seat.

For the next couple of minutes, as the plane climbed in altitude, Jamie wished she'd brought a little notebook or something to sketch with. This sensation was just too cool to be left to memory. Without much warning, the plane finally leveled out.

The plane almost seemed to stop and it felt as if the atmosphere in the cabin became weightless. Like a curious child on a field trip, Jamie leaned against the glass and looked downward. She breathed in deeply. It wasn't a gasp, but something softer and gentler. Whatever it was, it filled her entire body.

The town of Pebble Beach, and the beach itself, was a crescent along the blue edge of the ocean. It wasn't tiny, like it would look from a higher altitude. The cars were still clearly defined. The people were small, distinct figures moving along the sand and the streets. It was better than being tiny. It still looked real, just miniature real.

"God, this is amazing," Jamie said out loud, although Scott couldn't hear her. The plane, now that it was level, felt as if it was coasting like a kite. Along with the purring of the engine, Jamie could hear the wind whizzing around her. Everything was so overwhelming, she forgot to worry or be scared. Besides, she was too busy thinking, as usual.

She thought about how this summer was small. On the ground, it felt huge, but really, it was just a moment in a series of moments. Life was so much bigger than lying on her bed in her room, falling into the void. It was bigger than Pebble Beach and much bigger than Jamie herself.

And the thing was, it didn't feel bad to know she was so small. It felt magnificent.

She might forget to write it down. She might forget how scared she'd been at first. She might even forget Scott, someday. But she'd always remember being here, on top of the world.

Incidentally, for the moment, she forgot to think about Ethan altogether.

Walking across the small airport parking lot, Jamie looked down at her feet. She could feel Scott's eyes on her every few steps. When they got to his old Volkswagen convertible, he opened the passenger door for her and closed it behind her. Then he walked around the driver's side and got in. Scott put the key in the ignition but didn't turn it. He spun around to face her instead.

"You hated it."

Jamie was so surprised, she gave a start. She'd been off in her own world, still absorbing everything. But now she looked Scott directly in the eyes.

"Are you kidding? I *loved* it."

Scott's mouth tilted up in a smile. "Really?"

"It was . . . it was . . ." Jamie let out a breath and flung up her hands.

"Indescribable, huh?"

Jamie laughed. She'd forgotten what it felt like to do anything without thinking it through, even laughing. She felt free, like she could finally focus on the bigger world that existed just beyond herself.

"Yes, exactly."

Scott looked so pleased that Jamie wanted to hug him for caring so much whether she'd liked it or not.

She didn't fight the urge. Jamie threw her arms around him and squeezed. "You're the best guy I ever slapped in the face," she said with a wide, gleeful grin.

Scott laughed, blushing. "You could probably make it up to me."

Jamie didn't wait. She leaned toward him and kissed him on the lips. She basked in the pure pleasure of kissing someone she really liked. Someone who maybe wasn't the one. Or maybe was. Someone who could do something she couldn't do. And he'd wanted to share it with her. Somehow, that felt right to Jamie. Maybe that's what it was all about, after all.

Chances were, she and Scott wouldn't last forever.

But Jamie didn't really mind.

29

Kelsi shook Ella awake, claiming that they needed their last napoleons of the summer. Covering her eyes with her pillow, Ella pointed out that there was still a week left before they had to return home.

"But you know how it is," Kelsi insisted, tugging on Ella's arm under the sheets. "You think you have all this time and then all of a sudden, we're getting gas at the BP on our way back to Connecticut. Come on, El."

Ella let out a groan. Didn't Kelsi know that deep sleep helped you forget things that had happened, like, forty-eight hours ago? Didn't Kelsi have anything she wanted to forget?

Ella let her sister pull the sheets down and then slid out of bed. "I gotta take a shower," she said as she moped her way down the hall, her thin cotton boxers clinging to her butt.

"Fine," Kelsi said impatiently. "I'll be over at the picnic tables."

She padded past Ella in the doorway and headed down the corridor. Ella watched her disappear through the front door, then checked the clock in the hallway. It was 11:24 A.M. At least it wasn't too early.

When she knew Kelsi was out of earshot, Ella trudged into the kitchen and picked up the phone, dialing Peter's cell number, which she'd memorized. She'd just make this quick call and ask him to meet her somewhere later.

The phone rang three times and then Peter's voice mail picked up. It was surprising he'd strung enough words together for the greeting: "This is Peter. Leave me a message."

Ella hung up before the beep. Leaving a message might make her sound like a loser. Didn't he have caller ID on his cell? Didn't he *want* to talk to her?

"You're supposed to be showering."

Ella whipped around to see Kelsi standing outside the screen door staring at her. Ella felt the blood rush to her face.

"Um . . ." She tried to think up a person she might have been calling other than Peter, but it wasn't necessary.

"Get moving, slacker," Kelsi said with determination. "I'm going to stand guard by the phone." She turned and sat herself on the stoop. Relieved that Kelsi seemed to be in a better mood, Ella slid down the hall and into the bathroom.

Underneath the showerhead, she scrubbed her skin raw, wanting to wash away all traces of the sludgy feeling she had inside. Ella craved Peter so much she felt almost sick. But since the other night on the beach, her desire for him had changed. It wasn't just purely physical anymore. Now she just craved being near him and wanted his reassurance.

Reassurance of what? she wondered, soaping up her arms for the third time. She squeezed some Body Shop sea mud scrub into her right palm and rubbed her hands together, then smoothed the cleanser onto her face.

Maybe she needed to know it had been worth it. Because after all the waiting and wanting, everything inside was telling her it hadn't been.

"Damn it." Ella scrambled to flush the mud out of her eyes, scrunching up her face. She felt uncomfortable all over.

Once she had patted herself dry with her king-size towel and gotten dressed, Ella put on her makeup and plopped into the car with Kelsi. "What do you want for your birthday this year?" she asked as they sailed down Route 41 toward downtown.

Kelsi shrugged. "You never get me anything for my birthday."

"Well, maybe I'm maturing," Ella said, feeling guilty for all the times she hadn't. Last summer, she had forgotten to even get her a card. Sometimes Ella really disliked how self-absorbed she could be.

Kelsi smiled and let out a slight snort. "Right, Ella. You've definitely grown by leaps and bounds."

"Oh, stop being sarcastic. Seriously, the napoleons can be my treat," Ella offered graciously. "I want to make up for last year."

"Mmm, I don't think I want napoleons anymore."

"What? God, Kels, you . . ."

"I want to go to the diner," Kelsi said as she carefully slowed down for a yield sign.

"What?"

Kelsi looked as if nothing would deter her or change her mind. "We can get veggie burgers."

Ella said the first words of protest that came into her head, crossing her arms stubbornly. "I hate veggie burgers."

Kelsi shrugged. "Fine, get a hamburger."

Damn. "Kelsiiiii . . ."

"What?"

Ella searched her brain frantically for the most persuasive way to talk Kelsi out of driving to the diner. Seeing Peter with Kelsi would be unbearable. And what if Peter said something to *her* about the other night? There was no way Ella could do it.

But she couldn't say that.

"You don't want to see him, Kelsi," Ella said sternly.

"Yes, I do." Kelsi gripped the steering wheel, determined to go through with this, no matter what.

"Kelsi." Ella slammed her palms against her thighs as Kelsi narrowed her eyes at the road. "Napoleons are tradition," she finally blurted out. It was a lame attempt to make Kelsi feel bad, but it didn't come close to working.

"We can have napoleons for dessert. I have to see him, El. I just have to."

Ella didn't know what to say to that. She couldn't blame her sister.

In fact, she could identify completely with everything Kelsi was feeling.

The same snooty girl from last time was at the hostess podium. She wore the same cool look and gave them a heap of attitude, as usual.

"Two, please," Kelsi said firmly, surprising Ella with the iciness in her tone. Kelsi was lots of things, but she was never rude or cold. The girl, whose name tag said "Brandi" (*of course she would be a Brandi,* Ella thought), led them to a nonsmoking table that was right on the dividing line with the smoking section. Ella thought about how Peter smelled of smoke. She began to crave a cigarette, but then pulled out a piece of gum from her purse and chomped away. She had to resist all kinds of urges for Kelsi's sake.

Kelsi scoped the restaurant for any signs of Peter, while Ella pretended to study her menu. She was desperately hoping he wasn't here. Then again, maybe if he were working, it would make Ella feel better. At least she'd know he'd had a good reason for not answering the phone.

A middle-aged waitress with an enormously poofy hairdo came by to take their orders. "Veggie burger deluxe," Kelsi said, "and a cranberry juice."

The waitress rested on a hip while Ella searched her menu. She always wanted at least four things and never could decide without scouring the specials a dozen times. "Greek salad," she said finally.

When they were alone again, Kelsi leaned toward Ella and whispered, "Oh my God. I just realized it. That's her."

Ella straightened her shoulders and looked around the diner, wondering what Kelsi meant. "That's her who?"

"The girl at the podium. *Brandi.*" She dragged out the vowels in "Brandi" disdainfully.

Ella looked beyond Kelsi's delicate frame, past the guy who kept checking her out, toward the blonde ponytail of Brandi. "What about *Brandi?*" She mimicked Kelsi's pronunciation to emphasize how annoying it was when her sister was cryptic. Also, if she acted annoyed, she wouldn't seem as guilty.

Kelsi rolled her eyes. "The girl. The girl Peter was with last night. It's gotta be her."

Ella looked at Brandi's back again, her cheeks hot. She looked down and grabbed a sugar packet from the container by the window. "Really? You think so?"

"I swear, I sensed something was up when I used to come in here, but I thought I was just being jealous." Kelsi seemed oblivious to Ella's tomato-colored face. "I should have trusted my instincts."

Ella's eyes darted to the right, to avoid looking at Kelsi *or* the wrongly accused Brandi, to where a long, rectangular window revealed a chest-high view of the kitchen. She could see one familiar, now white-aproned, torso moving about with a spatula. "Oh God," slipped from her lips before she could stop it. She looked at Kelsi, whose gaze immediately darted where Ella had been looking. But then their view was blocked by their waitress's full figure.

"Veggie burger, Greek salad," she announced, laying down the meals and some condiments.

Ella immediately tackled her salad with the vinegar bottle, shaking and shaking its contents all over the fresh lettuce leaves and feta cheese. When the waitress backed away, there was another person lurking around in the kitchen. A girl. Whoever it was pressed close to Peter. Her arm snaked out and a hand went below Ella's line of vision. However, the angle that the arm was at left little doubt that this girl was grabbing Peter's butt. Ella's legs turned to Jell-O, the kind they serve at diner salad bars. Peter and the mystery girl were rubbing against each other, only briefly, but intimately.

"It's Brandi in there. She's doing it on purpose," Kelsi

growled. Her eyes were glued to the spot and nearly popping out of their sockets. "Because I'm here." She laid her fork down. "It doesn't matter. I don't need to do this anymore."

Brandi apparently communicated something to Peter, who did a ducking motion and then his face was staring out at them. Ella and Kelsi. Kelsi and Ella. Naive vacationing sisters who had fallen prey to the same guy.

And then there was a whoosh of air at Ella's side. Kelsi had stood up and she was walking out of the restaurant. *Walking.* Not storming, not slinking. And her head was held high.

Ella's eyes had gone back to Peter, but the rest of her remained nailed to the seat. He disappeared from view, and then came toward her out of the kitchen's swinging door. "Hey there," he said, as he closed in on her.

"Hey." Ella's voice was tremulous. Her eyes moved beyond him to the swinging kitchen door. Brandi was just coming out again. She frowned their way and then walked back to her podium, glancing back over her shoulder twice.

"Where'd Kelsi rush off to?" Peter asked.

"Are you having sex with that girl?" Ella's words completely overlaid his. It wasn't calculated, but she still expected the question to shock him. It didn't. He tucked his hands into his apron pockets casually.

"Why?"

"What do you mean, why?" Ella was worried she might start to cry. She already knew the truth. He didn't have to say. Her voice came out all high and pinched. "I snuck around for you. I went behind my sister's back. . . ."

Peter gave the first sign of being uncomfortable. He shifted his weight and took his hands out of his pockets, placing them on the table in front of Ella.

"It's not a big deal, okay?"

"Right. Me betraying my sister for you is not a big deal at all," she retorted angrily.

Peter's big dark eyes widened. "Ella, we had a good time the other night. Let's just leave it at that, all right?"

Ella put her palms to her forehead. A good time. She remembered the night in the haunted house, how dizzy she'd been, how she'd thought about him and agonized over him. A good time.

She stood up on her shaky Jell-O legs. She scanned the table and remembered she hadn't ordered a drink. In the movies, if a guy insulted you, you dumped your drink on him. You didn't dump your sister's drink on him, especially when the sister was the one you had *both* insulted.

Ella opted for her Greek salad instead. She tipped the bowl toward him and slammed it against his chest.

She watched as Peter's face, for once, actually took on human, emotional expressions — shock, surprise, and fury.

"Now *that* was a good time," she said vengefully.

Then she trotted out of the restaurant.

Even as she walked away, Ella was keenly aware that she exuded about one-tenth of the dignity Kelsi had, and about half the class.

30

Beth pushed her money across the counter and plucked a pink ball from the basket of multicolored golf balls. The girl running the Circus, Circus! kiosk opened the cash register and gave her some change. She had bad hair and thick, outdated glasses and reminded Beth a little of herself in the fifth grade. Only this girl had to be at least sixteen. She talked to herself as she punched numbers into the cash register and separated the bills — they were low words that Beth couldn't make out. *Things could be worse,* Beth thought to herself. At least she wasn't working at Circus, Circus!, wearing huge specs, and talking to no one in particular.

She took her club from the counter and walked the few feet to Hole #1, The Giraffe's Neck. Minigolf was open until 11 P.M. and it was only 7:45. Beth wondered how many games she could fit in between now and then. She placed her ball on the center dot on the green. She took a second to breathe and get to that peaceful place she went to during lacrosse games, surfing, and badminton. Then she took aim.

But before she could pat the ball forward with her putter, Beth saw George out of the corner of her eye. She jerked the club as she turned and hit her shin rather hard. She let out a small cry of pain.

"Hey," Bad Hair Girl crooned, wrapping George in a hug as he leaned over the counter of the kiosk. Before Beth's eyes, they kissed loudly, complete with slurping sound effects.

Beth was too stunned to gasp. But then, she didn't have to because it wasn't George. She could see now — it was some other skinny, tall kid. It was Bad Hair Girl's boyfriend. God, even Bad Hair Girl had a boyfriend.

"Figures," Beth muttered to herself, turning back to her ball and giving it a tap. It went nowhere near the hole. It struck a wall to the right and bounced back at her, then rolled past her onto the sidewalk. She had to chase it. It raced her to a patch of grass and won. Beth picked it up and started again.

She was through two holes before she figured out that the throbbing in her throat was not an impending cold. It was the sour sting of disappointment. Beth realized she was expecting George to show up. She might as well admit that to herself now, so she could skip the specific disappointment of the minutes passing by and move on to a more general disappointment later, when the night was over. From tomorrow morning on, she could wallow in disappointment on a more cosmic level — once he was gone.

This was the worst game of Beth's otherwise stellar minigolf career. She took six shots to get the ball in the hole at the Dolphin's Fin, which was way over par. She was bordering on short-shorts-wearing–bimbo-caliber skill. She looked over her shoulder several times to make sure no one was close enough behind her to notice how much she was sucking. She thought about marking a fake score on her card just to make herself feel better. As if that would work.

The final hole was an extra — Hole #19. It was the traditional Clown Face. There was no body, just a huge face and mouth, which opened and closed at irregular intervals. If you managed to get your ball across a little bridge and in between the lips before they snapped shut, you won a ticket for a free game.

Clown Face was Beth's personal nemesis. Whether she walked away from Circus, Circus! happy or sad often depended on whether or not she made the hole, which she did about thirty-five percent of the time.

She took aim, took the shot, and watched it sail in, hitting the clown's fluorescent pink epiglottis on the way down. She observed it without the least amount of satisfaction, but with a certain amount of surprise. It wasn't supposed to be her night. Then she scanned the area of the course one more time, just in case George had shown up while she wasn't looking.

She walked to the kiosk, where the girl and her boyfriend were talking in low voices by the cash register.

"I got a free game," Beth said woefully. The girl didn't bother leaving the kiosk to check Clown Face. She grabbed a ticket out of the cash register door and started writing something on the back.

"I'll just play now," Beth corrected her. The girl put the ticket away and smiled at her.

"Sure, just pick another ball."

"I know." Just because the girl had a boyfriend, she thought she knew everything. Beth grabbed a green one this time and headed back toward the soda machine. She fished three quarters out of her pocket and dropped them into the slot, hitting the big square button for the flavor she wanted. She then walked back to Hole #1 and began another game with her new best friends — green ball, golf club, and Mountain Dew.

When Beth got home, the windows of the house were casting squares of light on the grass. She'd played five games, two of which were free, thanks to Hole #19. George never showed up. There had been a group of drunk twenty-somethings killing time, and a lady with a pink hat and yellow glasses who'd played three holes and left. But her best friend didn't come by to apologize for deserting her.

Opening the screen door, Beth prepared herself to confront George. She'd act casual. She'd pretend she hadn't noticed that he'd been avoiding her. They could even spend their last couple of hours together pretending everything was normal. And who knew? Maybe to George, things *were* normal. Whether she'd kick his skinny ass if that were the case, she didn't know.

Her parents were in the living room watching TV. "Hey, guys." She gave them a little wave as they both looked up from the couch, then continued down the hall. George's door was open, but his light was off.

"Where's George?" her dad called to her back.

He wasn't here.

"I dunno, Dad," she said, trying to sound as if she couldn't care less where he was. She couldn't believe it. It was *unbelievable.* Her temples throbbed. He was still out! On his last night! Without her! She spun around and headed back out the front door.

"I'm gonna go out and look for him. See you later," she called out her to her dad in her most normal-sounding voice. But she wasn't going to go find him. Instead, she walked around the side of the house and then toward the ocean. When she got to the edge of the beach, Beth sat hard on the grass, her legs stretched out in front of her.

He was leaving tomorrow.

She was so anxious, she couldn't sit still. Beth stood up and paced along the sand. She had to do something with her nervous energy. She walked toward the next house over, to the hammock where Ella liked to lie. She pushed it a few times like a swing, hard, so that it almost flipped. Then she slung one leg over the side and climbed on. She pulled her arms around her chest, and rested her hands on her own shoulders, hugging herself. Then Beth felt all her emotions rush out of her like an avalanche.

The crying came out in little wheezes. Beth scrunched up her lips tight so she wouldn't sob, but she couldn't help it. She was doubled over and sobbing like a huge loser. She rubbed the tears off as fast as they came, to hide the evidence from herself that she was actually this upset over George. Her sniffling and the throbbing in her head helped to drown out the sound of footsteps in the grass.

"Beth."

"Oh my God," Beth shot straight up, sending the hammock swinging forward so that it almost dumped her onto the grass. Her reflexes were good enough to keep her on, but not by much. She stared up at George as he got closer and farther away and closer again, until he reached out a hand and stopped the swinging.

"Are you okay?" he asked, rather softly.

She rubbed at her face, wondering if there were still any more tears left on her cheeks. "Yeah," she answered while trying not to sniffle. "You just scared me."

"Scoot over," George said. Beth stayed where she was but he sank down next to her and pushed her with his body so that they were hip to hip, half sitting, half lying crosswise on the hammock. He didn't say anything and Beth just stared ahead, dazed.

"Why are you crying?" George finally asked, point-blank.

Beth took a deep breath. "I've got a raging case of PMS."

George offered her a pained smile. "Right." He got only slightly less phobic than most guys when it came to periods.

"What, you don't think I'm girly enough to get PMS?" Immediately, Beth was back to being angry. Her feelings could be turned on and off like a light switch.

George dropped his head into his hands. "I'm sure you are."

Beth snapped her lips shut. What was *that* supposed to mean? George continued, "I don't think that's why you're crying, though. I think you're crying because I've been such an asshole."

Beth kept her mouth shut and listened to her friend explain.

George rubbed his fingers along the crisscrossing rope between his knees. "Maybe that sounds cocky. That you'd be crying because of me."

Beth didn't say another word.

"Look, I don't blame you if you hate me. I came home tonight after I thought you'd be asleep. But your dad said you'd gone out to look for me, and that made me feel like a bigger asshole than I already did." He cleared his throat. "Which is hard."

Beth wrapped her arms around herself again. "You waited until you thought I was asleep." She was so incredibly angry.

"I was just freaked out." He clasped his fingers together and cleared his throat again. "I've been really scared."

Beth watched George's eyebrows lift in his worried way. They moved down and up with the beat of his thoughts. It made it easy to feel for him. Beth wanted to know what he was scared of, but she didn't feel like even asking him any questions. Finally, he spoke again.

"I'm really sorry about what . . . I . . . did . . . last night."

A sigh made its way out of Beth's trembling body. She could feel the tears creeping back out again from where they'd been hiding. "You're sorry?"

"Yeah. I really am, Beth."

He didn't seem to realize how hurtful his "sorry" was. "Sorry" he'd kissed her? George was looking at her with his big, apologetic eyes, as if being forgiven was the most important thing in the world. Beth wanted him to not be sorry. And at the same time, she wanted him to be sorrier. She felt all screwed up.

"If you're gonna apologize, why don't you say you're sorry for making me feel like I don't matter anymore," she said, letting her tears fall. "That's what you should really feel sorry for."

George moved closer to her and put his arm around her. "What do you mean? You matter."

"Not since Cara."

"Cara?"

Beth nodded and sniffed.

George tightened his grip around her shoulders. "Cara's nothing compared to you. She's just some girl I met this summer." Beth shook her head, mostly to herself. "Oh shit, Beth. Cara?" His voice had the awed tone of a person discovering some vast secret. "I made you feel that way?"

Beth shrugged. The whole conversation was becoming humiliating.

"Beth, you're my best friend," he whispered, close to her ear.

She waited for a long time before she said, "Still?"

George pinched her shoulder. "Yes, you idiot. What the hell?"

Beth couldn't help the smile that crept onto her lips. She felt like a three-year-old being bribed with candy. With a gentle motion, George sank back sideways onto the hammock and pulled her with him, so that they were both lying there scrunched up against each other.

Beth felt a huge weight lifting off her chest. Suddenly, lying next to him felt comfortable again. They could be Beth and George, best friends again. She sank into his body and let out a deep breath.

They lay in silence for a long time. The minutes ran by and they didn't move, until it had to be almost midnight. Beth felt herself nodding off to sleep but she didn't want to get up and go inside. She wanted to stay with George as long as possible, so she didn't move a muscle.

She was already half dreaming when George brushed her arm and said, "Do you know you have really soft elbows?"

It barely registered before she sank into sleep.

Beth opened her eyes, surprised to see that it was still dark. She felt like she'd slept for hours and that it should be morning. She wondered if her parents were up and worried about where she and George might be. Trying not to wake George, she shifted to look over her shoulder toward the house, and breathed a sigh of relief. All of the windows were dark. Clearly everyone had already gone to sleep.

As she shifted back down beside George's body, she felt him stir. Not so much because he moved, but because she was so close to him she could feel his breath, and the pattern had changed. She let his breaths land on her cheek, and then gently turned over to look at him. He was staring back at her.

Her skin went prickly, right away. George reached out his hand and touched her arm, her back, her face. The whole world seemed to slow to the rhythm of his breathing. There were only inches between their mouths and then, before Beth knew it, their mouths were touching — lightly, almost teasingly. George very softly pressed his lips against Beth's. He kissed just her upper lip, then rubbed his cheek against hers. Beth rubbed back. It felt playful and warm. Slowly, George traced the shape of Beth's mouth with his finger, then pulled her in close and kissed her fully, as he had the night before. But this time, kissing George didn't feel surreal or crazy. It just felt right.

Finally, he pushed back to look at her. "Is this okay?"

"Yes," Beth said.

"Good." He kissed her again, wrapping his arms around her back. When George pulled away, he stroked her hair. "Bethy," he whispered. "I've wanted to do that for so long."

Beth couldn't help but smile. "So what took you so long?" she whispered back.

"Me?" She could see George's familiar, lopsided grin in the darkness. "I was waiting for *you*."

Beth just laughed and rested her head against his chest, listening to his heartbeat. His arms were still around her. They were quiet for a moment, and then George spoke quietly, his lips brushing her ear.

"This is perfect. This is the way it should be."

"I know," Beth murmured. "Can we just stay like this forever?"

"Sounds like a plan." George's lips tickled her ear again.

Beth stretched like a cat, feeling deliciously aware of every part of her body. She could see it now, like a backward vision. Like she could predict the past. She could see all the things George had done that showed her how he felt. She'd just been too caught up in her own drama to realize it.

She nestled in closer to him, and buried her head deeper into his chest, marveling at how safe and happy she felt in his arms. George lifted her face and kissed her gently, and she let herself kiss him back, again and again, as many times as she wanted. They stayed that way until dawn, when it was time for him to go.

31

"You have any more bags that you want me to take out?"

Jamie glanced up from her bed, where she sat zipping the last of her luggage — a blue knapsack she'd stuffed with flip-flops, her sun hat, and a stack of paper, pens, and pencils. Uncle Carr was standing in the doorway wearing an orange sun visor and holding a duffel bag.

"I've got this one," Jamie said, allowing a smile to grace her face. "Are we leaving soon?"

"As soon as everyone else gets moving."

Jamie nodded. Her uncle and aunt liked to bring up the rear every time the Tuttles left Pebble Beach. Truthfully, Jamie liked it, too. For them, it was about tying up loose ends, but for Jamie, it was about making the good-bye longer. And she was a sucker for long good-byes.

"It looks like Beth is just about packed up," Uncle Carr said, disappearing into the hall.

Jamie pulled her knapsack onto her back and squeezed out

the screen door behind him, into the front yard. She placed her bag in the backseat of the green Jetta and gave the door a gentle shove. Across the dirt road, she could see Ella, Kelsi, and their dad going through similar maneuvers with their own luggage. Beth was at the picnic table in front of her cottage, her chin in her hands. Her feet were swinging and tapping underneath the bench.

As Jamie crossed the lawn to reach Beth, she pulled her thin, gray, hooded sweatshirt tighter around her front. There was a breeze coming off the water today that reminded her that September was around the corner.

"Hey," she said, sliding onto the bench beside Beth. "You should really try not to look so excited to leave us." Beth eyed her quizzically for a moment, then looked at her tapping feet and stopped them, a sheepish smile on her lips.

"Sorry."

"It's all right."

"I'm just excited to get home," Beth said with a happy sigh.

"I know."

Jamie knew the feeling too well. Beth had spent the last week bouncing around like the whole town was too small for her, spacing out at dinner, smiling at random moments for no reason. Her weird behavior had launched Ella on a crusade to pull out of Beth exactly what had happened between her, George, and Cara.

Ella was, of course, impossible to resist. Beth had confessed all to her one night. And since she'd entrusted the secret to Ella specifically, everyone — including all the uncles and aunts — knew about it now. So nobody blamed Beth for wanting to get back home, least of all Jamie.

"Did you call your mom?" Beth asked then, still smiling dreamily.

"Yeah," Jamie nodded, smiling. "It's so weird to think that by dinner I'll be back in the house. I think she's really happy."

"I'm sure." Beth ran both hands through her hair, making it stand out from her head like a tent. None of them, except for Kelsi, had showered this morning. They'd been out too late sitting on the beach, drinking the last of the family's beer and talking non-stop. And Jamie had been out latest of anyone. She and Scott watched the fire burn itself out after everyone else went home.

Around two, Scott had walked her to her door, and Jamie had kissed and hugged him good-bye. She'd gone to bed with a little ache in her heart, expecting to miss him this morning, but she didn't. Leaving the beach was always bittersweet. But this year it felt sweeter than usual.

"I'm ready to go," Jamie sighed, still feeling the little pinch in her chest that wasn't because of Scott, but just because of things ending.

"I think we all are." Beth was staring over Jamie's shoulder, and Jamie turned to follow her gaze. Ella — in sweatpants and a T-shirt — was hauling the last of her suitcases into the trunk of her dad's car, blowing bubbles with her gum.

"Do you think Ella's okay?" Beth asked at the same time the question ran through Jamie's mind. It had been hard to miss over the past couple of weeks, the way Ella seemed much more contemplative and quiet. She no longer initiated going out and dancing at Ahoy, and spent lots of time chilling with Kelsi.

Jamie shrugged. Neither of them knew what it meant or where

it had come from. It was just there. And the weird thing was, Kelsi was the one who'd broken up with her townie boyfriend — but she wasn't letting it get her down. She, in fact, seemed more spirited and confident than ever. It was a little bit like the sisters had taken on different qualities from each other. In a good way.

"Beth, time to go." Beth hopped out of her seat so fast at the sound of her mom's voice that she almost fell back onto the grass. Jamie snorted.

"Love you," Beth said, wrapping her arms around Jamie and squeezing her. "I'll see you at Thanksgiving."

"Yeah. Time is going to fly by," Jamie said, holding on tight. "Hey, good luck with George. Not that you'll need it."

Beth pulled back and grinned at her, then jogged across the lawn to Ella and Kelsi and their dad, and to Uncle Carr and Aunt Claire. Jamie walked over to stand beside Ella. They all waved as the car pulled away.

"That's our cue to exit," Kelsi said, shoving the last of her things into the backseat. "Daddy, what are you waiting for?" She disappeared into the house, following her father. Ella leaned back against the car, her arms over her chest, smiling at Jamie. She wasn't wearing makeup this morning, and Jamie couldn't help but notice that she looked more gorgeous than ever. She wondered if she should tell her that. Maybe she should confess how one day Ella was going to be a heroine in one of her novels. That might cheer her up. But Jamie opted to be funny and lighthearted instead.

"The boys of New Canaan will be happy you're back."

Ella shrugged. "I think I'm taking a break from boys."

Jamie studied her face. She couldn't tell if she was joking or not. "Really?"

"Really." Ella laughed at Jamie's expression. "Just for a while, anyway." Ella gave Jamie a big hug, just as Kelsi and her dad emerged from the house. Jamie and her uncle and aunt stood back as the girls piled into the car and slammed the doors. They left dust behind them the same way Beth had a few minutes ago, and then they were beyond the line of trees — just a sound of an engine. And then soon even the engine sound was gone. To Jamie, the whole place sounded quieter than it had all summer.

"Well, let me just get the kids and we can be off." Aunt Claire turned and headed back toward their cottage. Uncle Carr went back to the Jetta and rearranged their luggage in the obsessive way that dads do.

Jamie shuffled on the grass for a few seconds and then aimlessly walked around the side of the house and out into the backyard. A knot of seagulls had collected over the finger of water behind the cottages, apparently chasing a school of fish. Jamie watched them and wondered if she'd see the same birds next year. And that made her wonder: What would *she* be like in a year? She guessed that she'd still be the same Jamie. But knowing how quickly things could change over the course of a few months, she knew that she would be different, too.

"Jamie, why don't you go check your room really quickly to see if there's anything you missed," Aunt Claire shouted from the deck.

Jamie trudged back up the lawn and into the cottage, making her way through the den and down the hallway. She walked into her bedroom and sat on the bed, looking around. Half purposely, she *had* forgotten something. She let her eyes skip over it a few times, and then finally, focused on it.

213

The photo of Ethan was still stuck in the corner of her mirror, tucked tightly between the wooden frame and the glass. She'd planned to burn it, as some kind of symbolic girl power thing, but the time had gotten away from her. Quietly, she stood and slid it out of the crease, holding it on the corner with her thumb and forefinger. There were matches in the drawer in the kitchen. She could burn it in the sink. It would be a nice ritual.

But Jamie didn't move from her spot. She didn't really want to go find the matches, or want to burn the picture anymore. With her pinky she rubbed over the scar on Ethan's chin, just barely visible in the photo, thinking about all the things that she had loved about him. She tucked the photo into her palm and slid her hand into her front right pocket, leaving the picture there.

She'd put it in a box when she got home. She'd keep it in her closet somewhere — not anywhere important, but somewhere tucked away and safe. Jamie knew now that there were certain things you had to let go.

But that didn't mean they ever had to leave you.

Here's a peek at the sizzling sequel
to **Summer Boys,** *out in June 2005:*

Next Summer

by HAILEY ABBOTT

Ella spent the Fourth of July the way it was meant to be spent: lounging on the beach in a tiny bikini, Diet Coke in hand, Bain de Soleil–ing her skin toward a perfect tan.

Yesterday's rain had given way to today's bright heat, and Ella had staked out a perfect spot, where the soft white sand gave way to the harder-packed tidal sand. She could smell the clambake in the air, that hard salt tang that almost made her mouth water, and she didn't even like seafood. Families were setting up elaborate picnics up and down the shore, preparing for the fireworks later that night. Ella's tanning spot was smack in the middle of the commotion. She didn't mind. She liked to be where she could check out the entire beach.

Not that she was checking *anyone* out, Ella reminded herself as she applied another coat of Bain de Soleil. After her wild night with Inigo, she was reformed. No more boys this summer. Period. Even if being boyless was so darn . . . boring.

Ella noticed a set of boys passing by and pretended not to see them enjoy the way she greased up her legs, one shapely calf after the other. The old Ella would have made eye contact, maybe exchanged a few flirtatious words. But the new, post-Inigo Ella remained silent. Which wasn't to say she didn't love the way the tall one swallowed hard when she reclined against her towel.

Ella couldn't help it if she had a certain power. Kelsi was a brilliant student. When Beth performed some athletic feat, everyone talked about her talent. Ella's talent was making boys drool. Everyone had to be good at something.

Ella was turning over when she saw Beth walking up the shore with a lifeguard. As they drew closer, Ella appreciated the way the guy's shoulders moved, to say nothing of the six-pack he was sporting. She debated flinging herself into the water so he could rescue her, but discarded the idea. Daring rescues were romantic, sure, but she didn't like getting wet. All that seaweed and the possibility of jellyfish — yuck.

Beth was deep in conversation with the lifeguard. Her eyes were sparkling in a way Ella hardly recognized. When Beth finally looked away from the lifeguard and waved, Ella wiggled her fingers in reply, but continued to study the lifeguard. He was laughing, and Ella thought he had a familiar-sounding laugh. She tilted her head to the side and considered it. He had that dark curly hair and there was something about the way he —

Ella gasped out loud when she got it.

Pack on a muscled body and skin that actually tanned, and Beth was talking to a clone of George.

It would have been a little creepy if it weren't so funny.

"Hey there," Ella said, smiling her brightest smile, when Beth and the boy arrived at the edge of her towel. "I'm Ella," she told the hot lifeguard.

"Adam," the lifeguard replied. He was even cuter up close. Definitely a movie-star version of George.

"Bethy," Ella pouted. "How dare you hog the attention of the best-looking lifeguard on the beach?"

Beth rolled her eyes, but her cheeks were pink. "Adam's just helping me with my surfing, El. And there are plenty of other lifeguards. Go check out the guys at the station."

"Definitely," Adam said, grinning. Ella noticed, though, that his smile wasn't directed at her, but at Beth. "They could use a distraction. It gets crazy around here on the Fourth."

Ella turned to peer down the beach toward the big white lifeguard station, and shrugged. It seemed awfully far away, across a whole lot of hot sand.

"Are we going out later?" Beth asked, already backing away from Ella's towel.

"That's the plan," Ella said. Beth looked as if she couldn't wait to start her surfing lesson.

"I'll see you back at the cottages," Beth said, and then sauntered off with Adam. Ella smiled. If the situations were reversed, and she was parading around with a sexy lifeguard, Ella knew she certainly wouldn't waste her time on small talk with Beth.

Ella looked back toward the lifeguard station again. Lifeguards were, by definition, supposed to be in excellent shape. And lifeguarding indicated a certain interest in the welfare of others. That meant they were essentially good guys, right?

So really, she *had* to check it out for herself, just in case her future, serious, long-term boyfriend was there, waiting for her. Ella loosely tied her sarong around her hips. It perfectly matched her fire-engine red bikini. She adjusted her boobs with a few expert pats and she was prepared to go find herself the nice relationship she wanted.

Down near the lifeguard stand, Ella paused to consider her approach. It wasn't quite the all-you-can-eat hottie buffet that Beth had hinted at, but Ella couldn't complain. A tall, broad-shouldered blond guy caught her eye immediately. He had a square jaw and a confident grin that deepened when he saw Ella. She smiled back, but she didn't feel too excited. He was a little too . . . *wholesome*. Besides, Ella liked to be the blonde one in the relationship. It was just a quirk of hers that she couldn't explain.

The lifeguard sitting next to the blond, however, was a different story. At first glance, Ella had dismissed him. He had brown hair and eyes, which Ella liked, but he sat in a sort of careless way that gave her the impression that he didn't think anyone would be paying attention to him. But then he got up and climbed down to the sand in a few easy movements that changed everything Ella had been thinking about him. She took a second look.

He was a puzzle, that was for sure. When he hit the beach, the easy grace he'd displayed a few moments ago seemed to disappear, and he became a lean, lanky guy with shaggy brown hair. Nothing special.

Except . . . If she looked closely, there was a certain sexy, dark vibe going on that she couldn't resist. Even better, it was clear that he had no idea how cute he was. Ella could spot a winner when she saw one, no matter how awkwardly he carried himself.

She strolled right up to the lanky guy as if she were playing a game of chicken and she knew her opponent would definitely budge first. She made sure he got to enjoy the full effect of her red bikini and her curves. She watched his eyes travel over her and felt a little flicker of something in her heart.

This was the best part of meeting boys. Hands down.

"I'm looking for Adam," she said softly.

"Aren't we all," said the blond from up above. Ella smiled at him, but didn't linger, and quickly looked back at her hottie-in-hiding.

"He's, uh, giving a lesson," Lanky said timidly, as if he couldn't believe Ella was talking to him.

"Oh," Ella said very brightly. "With Beth, right? She's my cousin. We were supposed to meet up. . . ." She broke off, and flashed her sweetest smile at him. "I'm Ella, by the way."

He looked slightly stunned, but Ella took advantage of his reaction by moistening her lips with her tongue and ever-so-casually tousling her hair with her hands while arching her back. And if doing that thrust her breasts out, well, that was okay, too.

"I'm Jeremy," he said, never moving his gaze from her face, which kind of unnerved her. "Adam should be back in about fifteen minutes. You can wait here if you want."

"That sounds like a great idea. Why don't we wait together?"

His wonderfully dark eyes probed hers for a moment, then dropped back over her bikini quickly. Then he looked away and shrugged.

Ella smiled.

Finally, things were looking up.